Caden's Command

FINDING SUBMISSION DUET #2

Caden's Command

A BOLD SECURITY Novel

Zoey Derrick

COVER:
Cover Model: Christopher John
Cover Photographer: Lance Jones
Designer: Parajunkee Design

FORMATTING
Parajunkee Design

EDITING:
Mandy Smith - Raw Books Editing

:: created in the USA :::

For My Readers.

Thank you for your patience.
I hope that Caden's Command is everything
you've been waiting for.

OTHER BOOKS BY ZOEY DERRICK

I've come to you, Sir.
TO OFFER MYSELF TO YOU.
To give you my mind
and my **BODY** to cherish.
I've come to surrender to you, *Sir.*
To give you what you seek.
A submissive at your feet,
A LOVER FOR YOUR BED.

I cross the threshold into The Box.

My nerves are shot.

I can't focus on anything but the reason why I've come here tonight. The need to do what I'm about to do has been made abundantly clear.

Since I made this decision back in Sydney, I've found myself feeling more grounded and focused than I've ever been in my entire life. However, it doesn't mask the overwhelming fear in the back of my mind.

My last conversation with Caden, at the theater in Sydney, weighs heavily on my mind. The pain I felt when he walked away from me was almost unbearable. I knew I could call him, find him, and tell him everything had changed between us, but it didn't feel right.

I know what I'm about to do tonight is the only way to prove to him that this is absolutely what I want.

The lobby of the club is mercifully empty, except for Teddy and the girl who replaced Ashley for tonight. Teddy smiles at me as I approach to check in with the girl. She checks off my name and then the guy who stands guard near the door, locks them and saunters through the curtain followed by the girl at the podium. Her absence leaves Teddy and me alone in the lobby.

I pull off my jacket and Teddy's eyes scrutinize my naked chest. "You're really ready for this?" His voice is skeptical and I get the impression there is a lot more to Teddy than I've been made aware of. Who else would care enough to ask that question?

"As long as he doesn't know I'm coming."

Teddy smiles. "You're certainly going to give him a run for his money."

I give him a small smile as I kick off my shoes. "I hope so," I tell him softly.

"He doesn't know. Well, he didn't when he arrived, but I'm not certain where he's at inside the club. Ashley had made arrangements with him to scene tonight, but..."

"She'll stop him," I interrupt. "It was my idea. I figured that would be the easiest way to get him to the club tonight."

Teddy smiles wide. "Well, it definitely worked."

I head over to the coat room, hanging up my jacket and putting my shoes on the floor. Not knowing where he is inside the club has me worried and the reason I'm going in ready. The vision in my head as I made these arrangements was that he would be in the dungeon itself and not hiding in his private room.

To distract myself, I look over Teddy. He's a big guy, about my height, six-one, but he's burly in a way that I can understand as attractive. He has dark hair, almost black, with a little length to it and despite the burly aspect of his body; he's attractive with softer facial features and lighter colored eyes, maybe grey.

"I'm going to go in. I'll try and corral him to the middle of the club."

I offer a grateful smile at Teddy. "Thanks for all your help."

"Oh, I didn't do this for you, boy. I did this for him. He's been waiting a long time for this."

I tilt my head and narrow my eyes. "I've only known him for a few weeks."

Teddy shakes his head subtly. "He's been waiting for his 'one' for a long time and I think he found it in you."

My heart squeezes a little tighter, the fear and worry I had when I walked in the door kicks into hyper drive.

Submitting to Caden is everything I know I want and need in my life. That much has been made obvious, not only to me, but to those around me. While I realize that it's what I need, I'm unable to see beyond tonight or the next few months as I train with him. Anything beyond that will have to come in time. "I will do my best," I tell him softly.

"I know you will," Teddy says with a little more enthusiasm as he steps over to the curtain, pulling it open just a hint so I can see inside. "You're in luck." He smiles at me.

I smile nervously back at him and nod my head when he steps through the curtain into the club.

Alone in the lobby.

I pace back and forth while I rehearse what I want to say to him.

Then I panic when I realize that there is a chance I may not get to say anything at all. He may shut me down, walk away or worse, reject me. The fear rages through my veins.

I take a peek at what's going on beyond the curtain. I can see Raine and Dex talking though I can't hear them. I step through and my eyes travel around the circle of people standing in the middle of the dungeon. I see Teddy standing next to Caden, their backs to me.

"You may," I hear Dex tell Raine who jumps up slightly before grabbing the hands of the other two girls - Cotah and Ashley.

"I've never seen a bond like the three of them have with Will," Teddy says. "He's always in trouble and they always want to rescue him."

The four Doms standing around all burst into laughter at Teddy's statement and I step behind Caden.

"Sir?" I murmur.

Caden stiffens at the sound of my voice. A huge smile spreads across Dex's face and Derek's eyes go wide in surprise as he looks at me.

Just when I'm about to say something again, afraid that Caden doesn't want to turn around, he finally turns in my direction.

Our eyes meet, his steel grey to my brown, and Caden pulls a sharp breath through his teeth and instinct takes over when I lower my eyes to the floor.

"What are you doing here?" he asks sternly and the fear I felt before rages to the surface. Afraid this isn't going to go my way, I lower myself to the floor. This was my backup plan; prove to him this is truly what I want.

I sit back on my feet, place my hands on my thighs and allow my shoulders to deflate as this is my final hope to show him what I want.

He crouches down in front of me. "Answer me, boy. What are you doing here?" His voice is stern, commanding and compelling.

I take a deep breath, steeling myself for what I'm about to say. This is it, the moment I've been waiting for since I made this decision.

"I've come to you, Sir. To offer myself to you. To give you my mind and my body to cherish. I've come to surrender to you, Sir. To give you what you seek. A submissive at your feet, a lover for your bed. I cannot promise I will be any good at this, Sir, but I will do everything in my power to listen, to learn and to be everything you wish me to be. While I am everything I want to be. To please you, to serve you and be cherished by you, my Sir." I struggle to pull in a deep breath. It's out, I've said it.

His hand comes to my chin as he tilts my face up to look at his. I find it hard to pull my eyes to his, but in the end acceptance is what I need to see in his eyes. It's there.

"Are you sure, my dear sweet boy?"

I fight every muscle in my face to stop myself from smiling at him. His endearment for me is something I pray I never get used to. "I've never been more sure of anything in my life, Sir." A sense of home, life, desire, hope, and lust course white-hot through my veins.

"I prefer to be called Master," he states matter of fact.

"Yes, Master," I breathe.

He pulls in a deep cleansing breath. "I promise to nurture you, to cherish you, to train you and to push you to reach your goals. I promise to protect you and to honor you, both as my submissive and as my lover."

His words send me into a tailspin of emotion, everything from happiness, excitement, desire and then the underlying currents of worry and fear. The unknown stretches out before me in this one moment and I've never felt more prepared to take the steps necessary to start this journey with him.

"Stand, my sweet boy. I want you to stand for me now," he orders and I am no longer able to fight the natural urge my mind has to disobey him. With his hand still on my chin, I raise up, standing on my feet, looking into his eyes when his hand moves to cup my cheek.

Years of pain, heartache, loneliness and an unconditional need for acceptance and love overwhelm me and I lean into his touch.

"I've waited for you for a long time," he admits. His other hand comes to my face and he pulls me in for a strong, passionate kiss.

When his lips land on mine I feel like I've been found. No longer lost among the masses, but right at home where I need to be. The one person who can fill my every desire is kissing me to a round of applause from not only our friends but the entire dungeon. I've never felt happier than I do right this moment as I put everything I have into our kiss.

My mind comes back to me when I hear those closest to us getting a little louder than they should be and I blush uncontrollably. Caden, sensing my distress, pulls back from my lips. I can't help smiling at him before he releases me and takes my hand in his before turning around to face our friends.

Dex has a knowing smirk on his face as he wraps his arm around Raine. Derek is still a little stunned and I'm guessing that's not something that happens often with him. He's holding on to Cotah like he needs the support. Finally, I see Will snuggled into Teddy's side.

Teddy gives Caden a knowing nod and a smile. "Come here, brother," he says to Caden who embraces Teddy with his free arm.

Brother?

That term is tossed around so loosely anymore that it's hard to determine who's really family and who's not. The way Teddy said it tells me there is something more than just friends. They'd have to be step-brothers because they look nothing alike. Teddy has a more caramel, Mediterranean appearance to him and Caden is, well, white as can be.

"Don't you have some punishment to deliver?" Caden teases as he looks very pointedly at Will.

"Oh, I'm not in trouble," Will laughs.

"Not yet, boy." Teddy's stern tone is enough to silence Will and then Teddy laughs. "You can tell him why you were chained to the bar."

Will lights up and smiles wide, first at Caden then at me and back to Caden. "It was that or get my ass lit up for being a snitch."

I snort unintentionally and Caden's eyes dart to mine. I sober quickly.

"You knew, you obviously knew," he says pointing at Teddy. "You tied his ass up for it." Caden turns toward Dex and Derek. "Tell me, pet." My eyes dart to his, they're alight with curiosity and no malice at all. "Who all knew you were coming here tonight?"

"Ashley, Dex, Raine, and Teddy, Master."

"Uh-huh. I get the impression Cotah knew too." He looks at Dacotah who blushes red as a cherry and lowers her head into Derek's side. "That's what I thought."

"So why was I the only one left out of this equation? Well, besides Caden?" Derek asks looking around at everyone.

Dex bursts out laughing, "Because, you, out of all of us, are incapable of keeping a secret."

Derek scoffs and everyone laughs. The atmosphere turns toward old friends versus Tops and bottoms and I get the urge to just hang out with this group and talk the night away.

Caden squeezes my hand, drawing me out of my thoughts and my eyes to his. "We have a lot to talk about." His voice is soft, but there is still a hint of 'you're not getting out of it, not tonight' in his tone and I nod.

"I've got a pet to punish," Derek chides.

"But, Master, I was sworn to secrecy."

"It's true, she was," Dex agrees.

Derek has a mischievous smirk on his face when he says, "Secrets or not, someone should have said something." He laughs and leads a trembling Cotah off toward his private room as Dex approaches Caden.

"May I speak to your slave?"

"Always." Caden smiles wide and Dex slides in front of me.

"Well done, my friend."

On instinct my eyes dart to Caden who nods. "Thank you for everything."

Dex smiles, a playful friend side that I don't see that much anymore, makes an appearance, "I just want you to be happy. No matter what."

I look at Caden again. His warm brown eyes stare back at me waiting for my answer. "I am."

"Good, now, if you'll excuse me." I didn't expect playful Dex to stick around for very long, which it didn't, but he scoops Raine off the floor and she squeals as he hauls her off toward the private rooms.

Teddy and Will are all that's left and Caden turns to them. "Come over for lunch tomorrow?" Teddy asks Caden.

I'm surprised when Caden looks at me and asks, "You're not going home tomorrow, are you?"

"No, Master." I tell him with a small smile.

He turns to Teddy. "What time?"

"One is fine," he says nonchalantly and Will lights up.

"We'll be there."

"Good, now go talk to your boy," Teddy tells Caden and my heart starts pounding in my chest with nervous excitement as Caden pulls me toward his room in the club. We make it a few steps before he stops next to Ashley.

"Thank you," Caden says to her.

"For what, Sir?"

Caden nods toward me. "For Aryn."

Ashley gives him a small, sad smile. "You're welcome, Sir."

I'm not entirely sure what the sad smile was all about and I add it to the growing list of things to ask Caden about when the time is right. Between Teddy's comment and now Ashley's demeanor, there are some secrets here that I'd like to know about, but I don't expect my answers tonight.

Caden leads me down the hall; he doesn't say anything to me as he gets to his door and unlocks it, ushering me inside. The lights flick on and the door closes behind me.

I approach the bed but only get a step or two before Caden's hand grabs my arm gently and he spins me around. His hands slide into my hair, his eyes are intense, full of desire and lust and my breathing hitches when he brings his lips to mine in a hard, desperate kiss. My cock grows hard in an instant. I put my hands on his hips, holding myself up and pulling him into me, pressing my body to his. His hands slide down my neck to my shoulders and finally my biceps where he grips on to me, holding me to him.

His tongue is sliding along mine with more desperation than I've ever felt in my entire life and it pours into me. Making me useless and contrite. Making me hand over whatever control I thought I had in this kiss. My breathing is ragged, but so is his as he pulls back.

Both of us catch our breath for a moment.

I have no idea what is about to happen next, but I do know I'm ready for almost anything. I've made a list of things I refuse to participate in and a few that I'm unsure about. I knew before we could do anything, we'd have to discuss it, but I'm not sure that's what's on his mind when I look into his eyes.

"Everything okay, Master?"

Caden's lips spread into a wide smile and his eyes sparkle in the light of the room. "Perfect." I smile back at him. "You're just so beautiful; it's hard to take my eyes off you."

That, I can honestly say makes me blush.

I feel so flayed open. My heart beats in my chest for all to see and feel; my emotions are going a million different directions. I've never felt like I actually belong somewhere until this moment. And for the first time in my life, I no longer feel like something is missing. I'm amazed I was able to get all the words out. I said what I needed to say to him, to show him, to prove to him that this is what I truly want. I never expected that my promise of submission would bring me such a calm, peaceful feeling. It's humbling and it's heady.

"What are you thinking about, sweet boy?"

I smile. "You, me, us...about how I feel like I've found something I didn't know I was missing."

His hand comes to my cheek and he rubs his thumb quickly along my cheekbone before releasing me. "Good, that's how you should feel." He moves to sit on the chair, the same one he was in the last time I was in here. I just stand there, unsure what he wants me to do. He has a knowing look in the narrowing of his eyes. "Are you going to stand there all night?"

"No."

"No?"

"No, Master."

"Then where are you going to sit?"

"I don't know, Master."

His lip twitches. "Where would you like to sit?"

I let my feet guide me, going with my first instinct when I kneel beside him on the floor. His hand comes to my hair as he rubs his thumb along my scalp. I lay my head down on his thigh.

"Why did you pick that spot, pet?"

"It just felt right, Master."

"I like it."

I breathe a sigh of relief as I realize my instinct was right all along. It was right from the moment I met him. This is where I belong.

"*W*e have much to discuss, my boy."

"Yes, Master, we do."

"First, I need to know something." My voice is soft, overwhelmed by what happened here tonight. I feel so lost and unsure. Not something I'm used to. Sure, I've had several subs in my life before, but never have they come to me in the manner in which Aryn did tonight. I guess I shouldn't be surprised, he's full of them.

"Anything, Master."

I smile, despite the fact that he can't see it from where he's at; his head laying on my thigh, looking toward the bed. Though I can see his eyes, his expressions, and that is important tonight. "When did you make this decision? That you wanted to submit to me?" I ask the question that's been burning in my mind since I stood him up and kissed him back in the dungeon.

"Sydney, after you left me at the theater that night. I," he pauses, pulling in a deep breath before he continues, "I've never felt pain like that before, when you walked away from me. Knowing it could possibly be the last time I ever saw you, it was too much for me to handle."

"Then why didn't you come after me?" I know his answer, he was still working.

"Because it wasn't right."

I cock my head at him. "What do you mean?"

His lips twitch. "I knew I had to truly show you that I wanted what you were offering, that I was willing to take it to the next level. Simply telling you wasn't going to be sufficient for either one of us."

I smile wide at him, realizing that him doing what he did tonight was for my benefit but I believe he got exactly what he needed to out

of it too. It's one thing to decide you're going to submit yourself to someone, it's a wholly other thing to actually do it, show it, prove it. He's done exactly that. "Well, pet, I'm very glad you did."

"Thank you, Master."

"I'm pretty sure you're going to be better at this than you think," I tell him and he raises his head to look at me.

"Tonight, it's easy. I am desperate to prove to you that this is really what I want."

I stroke his cheek with my thumb. "You've already done that," I respond honestly.

"I also don't want to disappoint you."

"How would you do that?" I ask him with narrowed eyes.

"I don't know. I don't want to say something that will upset you."

"We don't walk on eggshells in this relationship, Aryn, not now and not ever. Communication is our number one rule. Failing to tell me something that you're thinking, concerned about or just curious about will have severe consequences," I tell him, though maybe a little harsher than is necessary. I can't do this with him without open and honest communication and while he's being open tonight, I have a feeling he will close up eventually. We all do.

"I understand, Master. But I also know it won't always be easy for me to do that."

"How do you know, my boy, when you've barely even tried?" I ask.

"Because I've never been one to tell anyone anything, everything. I've been alone in this world far too long." His voice trails off toward the end of his explanation. I knew this long before we got to this point. He's damaged and broken and I intend to do everything I can to heal him and bear the burdens for him. But that will have to come in time. While I want desperately to take everything away from him, to carry the weight of it on my own shoulders, I know he's not going

to give me that kind of power so easily.

"I want to discuss that some more, but I think maybe we need to discuss a few other things first."

Aryn nods his head and returns it back to my thigh. I return my hand to his hair, giving him the comfort of my touch and when I see his shoulders loosen up just a bit, I know that it's working. "Tell me, pet, what will your safeword be?"

He shrugs his shoulders. "I hadn't thought about it. I guess I just assumed you'd give me one."

"Ah, but you need to decide on something that, when said, cools everything off. I cannot pick a word for you that possibly means something to you. You need to decide on a word or thing that you hate and something that wouldn't be said during a scene or sex for that matter."

"How about something that means a little bit to both of us?"

I smile at his words. "And what would that be?"

"Hollywood," he states plainly.

My lips twitch with a smile and I nod my approval. "Hollywood it is then."

We sit in silence for a few minutes before he shifts himself to face me. His eyes are soft, almost content and I smile at him.

"I didn't expect you to be so quiet," he whispers.

"I'm still in shock, I think."

"Because of what I did tonight?"

I nod. "Of all the things I was expecting tonight, this certainly wasn't one of them."

"Are you disappointed?" His voice trails off and I see the concern he has when his eyebrows knit together.

"Not at all. It's a good feeling, I promise. I guess I was just taken off guard and that, my boy, is something that's hard to do."

He smiles wide. "Good, I'm glad."

I snort, "You know, you shouldn't be."

"Oh, and why is that, Master?"

"Because," I lean close to him, his scent is erotic and it goes straight to my cock. Realization slides over me- he's mine. "I don't appreciate topping from the bottom."

He blushes at me and I see the remorse in his eyes as he closes them. "I wasn't trying to top from the bottom, Master."

I put my hand on his cheek and tilt his head so his eyes can meet mine. "I know," I breathe and I urge him up higher, giving me a better angle to press my lips to his. There is a spark that ignites in me when he moans into my mouth as I claim his. The blood rushes in my ears, effectively deafening me as my heart rate increases. My cock hardens and what self-control I had starts slipping away.

Kissing him is a whole new experience for me. Kissing him now, knowing he's committed himself to being my submissive, sends a new wave of pleasure through me and I pull back reluctantly.

His eyes are closed and his eyelids are heavy as he fights to open them and look at me. When he does, I don a serious face. "I need to know your limits," I practically growl at him. It is taking every ounce of control I have not to tie him to the bed, to do something with him, anything.

"I don't do water sports."

I shudder. "That's a given. So are any other bodily fluids besides cum and saliva."

He nods and adds, "I'm not entirely sure how I feel about pain."

"As in, you don't want to experience it at all?" God, I hope not.

"No, just something I need to work up too," he tells me and I let out the breath I was holding. I'm not a sadist per say but some of my favorite toys are whips.

"That's to be expected. I didn't expect you to take a whip on our

14

first outing, but I will tell you that the whip is my favorite."

He swallows hard.

"Easy, my sweet boy," I tell him calmly. "I'd like you to do something for me." He nods, but it's subtle and reluctant. "I'd like it if you kept an open mind while trying new things and discovering what you like and what you don't like. I can assure you that unless you throw down something as a hard limit with valid reasoning, I'd really like it if you tried everything and then you can decide what works and what doesn't." I sit up a little straighter in the chair. "For example, if you find something that you don't like, it doesn't mean it falls on a hard limit, but it may fall into the punishment category."

He swallows hard again and lowers his eyes.

"Punishments are a necessity, pet."

"I know. I just don't like the idea of it."

I smile wide. "If you liked the idea of punishments, this can't work."

"I know, it's just so..."

"Degrading?" I ask and he nods.

"It seems that way now, but I assure you, they're never meant to degrade you. Take Will for example." He acknowledges me by turning back to look at me. "He is a social butterfly. He loves to talk to people and he especially loves those that are closest to him, like Cotah. One of the worst punishments Teddy can give him is what he did to him tonight. He tied and blindfolded Will to the bar tonight because if he didn't, Will's lack of filter would have, no doubt, ruined your surprise. So, Teddy tying him to the bar, unable to talk to anyone is pure torture to Will, but in the end, when Will was released?" Again he nods, acknowledging my question. "Did you notice how quiet he was?"

"I did." He cocks his head as if what I'm saying is making sense to him and I smile.

"He'd learned that he could have been a part of everything if he'd just learn to keep his mouth shut."

"So why doesn't he?"

I give Aryn a big, wide smile. "Because, that's exactly who Will is. Teddy will never dull that spark he has. In fact, Teddy thrives on it."

"So why tie him up?" He purses his lips.

"Because he knew that tonight was important to me, whether I knew it or not."

"I didn't tell Teddy."

"I know you didn't, Ash did. She had to. Teddy is Ash's mentor. He took her under his wing to train her and that's exactly what he's done with her. She's ready for her own Top, when she finds one," I tell him and I realize I've opened up an entire barrage of questions from Aryn about Ash and I guess now is as good a time as any to answer them.

Those questions never come. Though I can sense the wheels are turning, the conversation switches back to us rather quickly and I'm impressed. Though he does need to know about Ash and what role I had in her training, I realize this isn't entirely the best time to discuss it and so does Aryn.

"So, tell me, what are some things that you do like, my pet."

He gets a little more animated and excitement flitters in his eyes. The idea of punishment is never something any sub wants to talk about. They all know it happens, but I think the best way to handle them is to not know about them.

"I loved being tied to the bed, that night..." his voice grows soft, somber, "I'm really sorry about that."

"About what, boy?"

"When I ran out of here, after we, with Ash..."

"Apology accepted, but I will tell you now, that if you do that to me again, you will find yourself in a very unhappy situation."

"I understand that now, I just didn't know, or understand what it was that I was feeling at the time, I just..."

"Panicked?"

He nods.

"We all have our moments; which is why I've stressed communication to you. It's imperative that we discuss things. I cannot fix something I've done or am doing wrong if I don't know about it. I can't possibly understand what you're doing inside your head if you don't tell me. Though it may seem that way sometimes, I cannot read your mind."

"I promise to do my best."

I cup his cheek. "Your best is all I ask, my sweet boy."

I move, and Aryn shifts off me. I stand and offer him my hand. He takes it and I help him from the floor. "So you liked being tied up?" He blushes in response. "Good. What else?"

He shrugs. "I don't know...I liked watching Teddy with his whip, I liked when Mistress Milena used her flogger."

I smile. "That's a great place to start. Come," I command him and lead him toward the door. I open it, turning back to him. "The easiest way to know what you might like is to watch it."

I step into the portal and grab his hand, bringing him with me back toward the dungeon.

CHAPTER FOUR

Aryn

My nerves settle a bit when we sit inside the dungeon. I am surprised at how comfortable I feel when Caden sits on one of the bar stools. Once he settles, he opens his legs and with a gentle nudge, pulls me back between them. Then he wraps his arms around me, holding me to him. There's a warm comfort that slides through me making me feel safe and wanted.

To think, twenty-four hours ago I was single and alone, and now I feel like I've been consumed by the protective blanket being offered to me by him and it's the most natural feeling in the world.

My nervousness stemmed from the unknown of what was going to happen after I made my confession to him. I didn't know what he would do and while I didn't expect him to tie me to a cross and go to work on me, I was freaking out about that being the case.

No matter the amount of reading I've done about D/s relationships, I couldn't help worrying about the aspect of 'everyone is different'. Caden has proved to me that while he wants me as his submissive, he doesn't want to jump right in without first knowing everything about me that can make me tick.

"See anything you like, pet?" His voice sends a jolt through me, too consumed with my own thoughts and being in his arms. Though I manage to stifle the physical reaction, his arms tighten around me and his thumb rubs tenderly in a calming rhythm against my stomach.

My eyes roam the room. Teddy and Will have only just come out of their room. A couple of stations away from them I see Derek and Dex standing side by side. I follow their line of sight to Raine's nearly naked backside. She's spread wide on a St. Andrew's cross and Cotah is tending to her. Her hands gently slide up and down Raine's sides and I can visibly see Raine relax as the tension in her arms disappears.

My eyes continue around the room and while there are several other couples in the club, I don't know who any of them are. That is until my eyes land on Mistress Milena and her female submissive who is leaning over a padded table. Her arms stretched wide, her ass exposed to her Mistress who is yielding a flogger with falls significantly longer than what I've seen before. They're also thicker.

"What's that, in Mistress Milena hand?" I ask Caden.

"It's what it looks like, only the falls are braided. It makes for more of a sharp bite." Caden's sultry voice in my ear makes this implement sound like a handful of feathers.

Mistress Milena cracks the flogger and her submissive arches her back as the sound registers in my ears. My eyes widen and my pulse quickens. Looking more carefully at the submissive strapped to the table, I can see the red evidence of her Mistress's administrations against her back and I shudder.

"It's pretty intense. Often those who favor a single tail whip enjoy that kind of a flogging."

"The way that she, her sub, reacted, is that..."

"Everyone is different but in this case Carta, her submissive, enjoys immense amounts of pain. She's floating pretty high right now." He points toward them, "If you notice how her Mistress is very attentive to her after making her climb."

"Climb?" I ask.

"It's a common term, climbing the cross; it means something has hurt or happened that can pull a submissive out of their space. Whether it was intended by the Top or not is not always clear, sometimes Tops do it to keep their submissive in place for a while longer. To keep them from floating off too far too fast."

I shake my head. "I'm not sure I understand."

His tongue traces along my ear and his teeth nip at the lobe, shivers radiate and goosebumps fly across my skin. "It's impossible to explain, it's better when you experience it for yourself." He nips at my earlobe again before kissing that sweet spot just behind it and my cock twitches.

His hand slides up my stomach. The warmth of his hand is calming until his fingers brush over my nipple and every nerve ending comes alive. My entire body is electrified and I let out a gentle huff of pleasure.

"You like that, don't you, my sweet boy?"

"Yes, Master," I breathe and he flicks a finger across my nipple again. This time harder and I feel the slight stick of pain, but it only heightens the sensations wracking my entire body.

"Keep watching." His voice is a clear order through gritted teeth and I open my eyes, rescanning the room, looking for something to distract me.

Only my eyes land on Dex who has a wicked looking whip in his hand, curled up, resting. He talks with Derek while Cotah continues tending to Raine.

Dex uncoils the whip and I watch as he rolls his wrist. Testing the weight in his palm. Then he flips it backward and then forward. There is no audible crack when at the same time Caden pinches my nipple between his fingers. Sending a jolt of pain through my body and my cock throbs.

Dex repeats the process and Caden does his. With each kiss of the whip against Raine's ass, Caden finds a small way to inflict pain on me, like I'm feeling what Raine is feeling and my cock is nearly ready to explode.

Suddenly a loud crack makes me jump and my head snaps to Teddy and Will.

Will is clearly in his happy place despite the fact that Teddy isn't actually hitting Will. No, he's cracking the whip, sometimes close to Will, other times back by himself and it's sending Will into an obvious place of happiness and submission.

Teddy walks to Will and presses himself against Will's backside. If

I were closer, I imagine I'd hear Will's whimpers when Teddy's hand grips his hair and pulls his head back. Teddy places an aggressive kiss against Will's mouth, consuming him whole and his submissive turns to butter against the cross.

Caden's right hand comes off my chest and slides into my hair. His fingers give a firm tug and I shiver with anticipation.

My breathing quickens as Caden turns my head toward him, his eyes on mine. His eyes glisten with lust, a desperate level of it, unlike anything I've seen before when his lips slam against mine in the most earth shattering kiss I've ever felt in my life.

The entire club could be on fire and I wouldn't notice as Caden's tongue claims mine. My breathing stops altogether and my heart kicks up another notch.

My knees start to go weak as his hand tightens in my hair. His other hand grabs on to my hip, urging me to turn around toward him. In my lust crazed haze I somehow manage to do just that.

His hand on my hip digs into the soft flesh there as he pulls me into him, hard and tight. I feel his erection through his jeans pressing against my own and I want to lower myself to the floor right here and now. I want to feel his cock between my lips once again as I fight to catch my breath.

"Let's go," Caden breathes as he pulls.

Wait, what? I shake my head.

"Where's your shirt, shoes?"

It takes me a moment to catch up with him. He's pulling me out of everything I was just feeling and I'm thoroughly disappointed. "In the coat closet, lobby."

"Go, get it, and get dressed. Stay there."

Uh, "Yes, Master."

I can't hide my dissatisfaction. The idea and feeling that I've somehow managed to disappoint him washes through me like oil in

my veins as I walk toward the velvet curtain.

Not wanting to see the look of disappointment on his face, I don't turn back.

I do as he's asked of me. Pulling on my shoes and then my jacket, pulling the hood up over my head, desperately looking for someplace to hide, but the lobby is void of anything concealing and I fight the urge to push through the doors and leave.

The only thing that keeps me here is the fact that I promised him I wouldn't run again. Besides, I have nowhere to go. He'll track me down before I can manage to hail a taxi and before I can duck into the safety of the restaurant I was dropped off at to wait for one to show up.

It was a bad idea coming here without my own transportation, knowing full well that Dex would be busy with Raine tonight. He even argued against it, but I knew if I brought a car, it would give me an easy escape and I may not have done what I did tonight.

I fight the urge to pace the lobby.

It goes against my nature to sit still, to be so vulnerable and exposed and that is exactly how I feel right now. I want to scream.

As soon as I get to the point of feeling completely and totally uncomfortable, wishing I'd taken my chance to run when I first came into the lobby, Caden steps through the curtain.

There is an overwhelming look of approval on his face until he sees the stress in the creases of my forehead.

"Let's go," he orders as he steps to the door, pushing it open.

I lower my head and step through the doorway and out into the chilly night air of Nashville.

"Where's your car?"

I shake my head.

"I won't ask a second time."

Jesus, he's angry with me. What the hell did I do wrong? "I don't

have one. I don't live here, remember?" I snap.

"Watch it."

I bite the inside of my cheek to stop myself from snapping back at him. For all I know, I've done nothing wrong and his desire to leave has nothing to do with rejecting me and everything to do with wanting to be somewhere other than the club. I've officially made a complete and total ass out of myself.

"If you don't have a car, and Derek didn't know you were coming, and Teddy was here long before I was, how in the hell did you get here?"

I sigh, "I took a cab."

"You brought a cab to the club? Jesus, Aryn, you can't…"

"No, to the restaurant, the one down the street. I walked to the club," I explain somberly.

"How'd you plan on getting home?"

"By airplane."

This pulls him up short. "Where are you staying?" he says a bit softer.

"The Omni."

"Come on then," he says as he heads into the parking lot and I follow him.

I feel so, god, I don't even know what I'm feeling right now, but this certainly isn't how I pictured this night going.

He approaches a car, an SUV, a Lexus no less, and presses a button on his key fob. The back gate pops open and he throws his massive bag into the back. I shudder at the idea of what it is he has in there and then dread washes over me at the thought of never finding out what's inside it.

"Get in," he orders and it takes everything I have to stop. To ignore his order.

I don't say anything as he walks to the driver's door, out of my line of sight. My eyes dart around the lot. I spot Derek's SUV and I know I can't get back into the club; I can wait there or walk down the street.

"Aryn?" Caden snaps.

My head whips around to him. "What?" I snap back.

"Enough," his voice is softer now, finally realizing that I'm not going anywhere with him, not when he's acting like this, "what happened between the dungeon and here?"

"Nothing happened."

His eyes narrow, that Dom mask he wears so well slips on to his face.

I can no longer fight him. "One minute we were kissing, it was hot, it was heavy and then the next," I take a deep breath, "the next you're dismissing me."

He takes a couple of steps closer to me and I fight the instinct to step back from him. "I didn't dismiss you. I no longer wanted to be at the club with you."

His statement just proves my point and reinforces why I should have run when I'd had the chance. "I'm sorry, I shouldn't have come tonight," I mutter and start walking toward the street. Unfortunately I have to walk past him in order to do so.

He grabs my arm as I walk past. "Where are you going?"

His voice is eerily soft and I shudder. "To catch a cab."

"You most certainly will not."

I turn on him. "You don't want me here, the club is locked and my friends are inside for god only knows how long."

"Just a minute." He cocks his head at me. "What on earth gave you the impression that I wanted you to leave?" He pauses, scrutinizing me. "You crawled inside your head, you thought, god no, Aryn. I was not rejecting you, not at all. I just couldn't stand to sit there for

another minute. It was driving me insane to have you so close to me and there was nothing I could do about it. I wanted somewhere private."

My heart sinks into my stomach as I look at him.

"Aryn, I didn't want to stay at the club anymore, watching them, Teddy, Dex, Milena...don't you see? I couldn't keep watching them, doing what they're doing to their pets and not do that stuff with you."

"Well, I feel like shit," I mumble.

"You should."

"That's not fair," I protest.

"Neither is you hiding in your head."

"You didn't even give me a chance."

"I knew you'd made up your mind when I stepped into the lobby. You'd already assumed I'd changed my mind, you were listlessly roaming around in your own head about what happened in the bar."

"You were disappointed in me."

"Absolutely, but only because you could have asked me before you went into the lobby, you could have waited until I came into the lobby to ask me what my intentions were. As soon as I realized that you'd shot down that idea in favor of the worst possible idea rather than the idea that I simply wanted to be alone with you."

"No, I considered it, right before you bit my head off about the cab. At that point I dismissed it because you were so pissed at me." I pull my arm from his grip.

He doesn't hesitate in cupping my cheek in his hand. "I'm not pissed at you. Disappointed that you slipped into your head the way you did? Absolutely, but that doesn't mean this night needed to end. It meant that we had some talking to do, which I fully intend to do." I shiver from the cold as he speaks. "As soon as you're in my truck and out of the cold.

I nod softly and he releases me, but he doesn't move. He waits for my next move and though I don't want to fight with him anymore over my stupidity, I don't want to leave him either. I walk toward the passenger door. Once there I open it and climb in, huddling against myself.

A few heartbeats go by before he climbs in and starts the engine. He doesn't back out so we can leave.

"Why couldn't we have gone to your private room?" I ask him.

"Is that really where you want our first time together to happen?"

His question sends a shiver of desire through me and my blood pumps through my veins warming me up faster than the heat can. "No."

"Neither do I. I needed you out of the club because I can't have you there, it's a distraction."

"How so?"

He sighs, "Seeing them, the Tops, working over their bottoms only made me want to be working on you that much more. If we stayed there or went back to my room, I'd have all the equipment I'd need and you're not ready for that. I'm not even ready for that. There are a lot more things we need to discuss before we can even begin to play in the club."

I lower my head, shame and embarrassment consuming me like a blanket as I realize he's absolutely right. "I'm sorry, Master."

His hand pushes my hoodies off my head and places his hand on the back of my neck, urging me to look at him and I do. I can't hide it, the shame, embarrassment and worry I feel is cemented in my eyes, in the creases of my forehead. "I know, pet. But this is truly a good lesson for you."

"How's that?"

"Communication. Asking the questions you have, when you have them, rather than sliding into your own mind. If you ask me, I will

tell you, always. But I can't tell you the answer when I don't know the question. Understand?"

I nod. "Yes, Master."

He smiles at me and pulls on my neck, pulling me toward him so that our noses are practically touching each other, his eyes on mine, "Good," he breathes right before he captures my lips with his. His kiss instantly sends me right back where we were before he wanted to leave.

*N*ormally I would be happy that an experiment worked. I knew when he walked away from me, dejected, that he'd assume the worst of the situation and I wanted to teach him a lesson in communication. No, I won't punish him for it, this time. I think he learned his own lesson in the fact that communication is everything between us.

I pull out of the club's parking lot and head toward his hotel. I'd had every intention of finishing what I'd started with him tonight and I still plan to do that. I've waited way too long for this. I need this as much as he does.

"If I asked you to tell me what's scorned you to make you think the way you do, would you tell me?" I ask him.

"I will, eventually."

"Why not right now?"

"Because there isn't enough booze in the vehicle and the trip to my hotel room isn't that long."

"Fair enough, but I will be asking again, before you leave Nashville."

He nods his understanding as the light changes and I press on the gas pedal.

We ride in silence until he breaks it as we draw closer to his hotel in the Broadway area. It's not far from the club and yet on the other side of town from my house. I figured wherever he was staying was closer than my house and that is the only reason I'm bringing him here. I have every intention of staying here with him tonight. What happened tonight, not just what happened as we were leaving, but his confession, has him raw and I won't leave him, not until we've had a little more time to talk.

"Why are we going to my hotel?"

"Because it's closer than my house."

"Oh," he says but I look at him in enough time to see his lips turn up in a smile. Good, I haven't lost him completely tonight. "How come you haven't asked me how long I'm staying in town?"

I give him a sideways smirk. "Because I don't want to watch the clock. I don't want to know how much time I have before you're going to leave me."

His smile grows a little wider and I can see the blush in his cheeks in the faint street lights as we draw closer to his hotel.

"Regardless of when you're leaving, it's too soon," I tell him and he turns his head toward me. "Or, I can make you stay longer."

His shoulders shake with silent laughter, almost as if he's daring me to force him. I will, if it's necessary.

We pull up to his hotel and I pull into the valet area. He climbs out and I follow, handing the valet my keys as I pop the back gate of the truck. I need my bag. If for no other reason than the fact that I have some things we may need and I have a change of clothes in there as well.

I catch Aryn's eyes widen when I pull the big play bag from the back and I smirk. Yes, my sweet boy, there are lots of toys in here for you, but not for tonight.

Aryn showing up at the club and declaring his intentions to me threw me off guard because I never expected it to happen, ever. Let alone have it happen so soon and more importantly, when I least expected it, like tonight. I almost feel like a duck drowning because I haven't even a clue where to start with him.

"Lead the way," I tell him and he hesitates. "Would you prefer I go?"

He shakes his head. "No, I want you to stay."

"Then?" I tilt my head toward my shoulder, appraising him, trying to read him.

"I wasn't prepared for you to come here. I thought we'd go back to your house." He hesitates a moment. "I don't have anything here."

I adjust the bag on my shoulder and he catches my drift and with a smile he turns to the sliding double doors of the Omni.

I follow behind him as he leads me toward the elevators and I can't help watching him. He slides his hood down once we're inside and his confidence returns with each step he takes. I only wish I felt so sure.

With previous subs, I knew what I wanted and went after it. With them I could lay down my ground rules and learn if they had a few of their own and it was easier from there. Of course, there was that awkward 'getting to know you' phase, but for the most part, the subs I've played with have had a mentor, like Teddy, who would vet me before I could even talk to their submissive trainees. Those first few sessions were always followed with their mentor watching over and guiding on certain tells they knew about, this also put the subs at ease knowing someone was watching over them.

Aryn is the exact opposite of all of that and it scares the hell out of me. This is new, different and despite my fears, exciting. Aryn isn't a sub with a predetermined list of rules or hard limits. There's no pre-arranged script for how the night is going to go. Plus, there is what makes me smile. If I want to have sex with him, I can because he's mine.

Aryn presses the up button on the elevator and when it arrives, a couple leaves before we step in, trapping us both inside the tight space. The moment the doors close, I pounce on him, pressing him against the back wall. My aggression surprises him momentarily before he settles into my kiss. I hold him against the wall, my tongue sliding along his as the numbers chime as we climb, though it's far too short when the doors chime and the elevator slows, signaling their intent to open and I pull away from him.

His breathing is audibly erratic, matching my own and I smile at him. He blushes and I stroke my thumb along his cheek. "I like this."

"It's a new novelty to me too, Master," he whispers.

He leads me into the hallway and down about halfway before we get to his room.

The Omni is a nice hotel, a little on the pricey side for what it is. Aryn opens the door and he holds it open for me. I give him a reassuring smile as I step inside the tiny, king-sized room.

The accommodations are much smaller than the last hotel room I saw him in and it only takes me a moment to remember why. He was working then, now he's not. He's paid for this on his own and I bite back any retort I had on the tip of my tongue about his room.

I don't even know why or how it is that I got so pretentious.

"It's not much," Aryn says behind me. "But it was all I could find at the last minute. Apparently there's some big event here in town this weekend."

I turn toward him, setting my bag down on the bed. "It's perfect."

He nods, but it's an uncomfortable nod.

"Come here," I tell him and he comes over to me. I grab the zipper of his hoodie and pull it down. His chest glistens underneath, inviting me to touch it. Right now, I really just want him to be comfortable.

He slides the hoodie off his shoulders and he kicks off his shoes. "Can I get you anything?"

"Water would be great."

I have to admit, I don't know if I've ever felt this nervous since Shelly or maybe even when I lost my virginity. I want so much to happen tonight and yet I haven't a clue where to start. That coupled with everything else tonight has me completely off my game and I don't like it.

Aryn hands me a bottle of water from the mini-fridge. "Thank you."

"Of course." He smiles and opens his own bottle, drinking down half of it before he puts the cap on it again. "So, what's in the bag?" he asks with a playful smirk on his lips and I can't help but smile at him.

"Are you sure you want to know?" I say mischievously, of course that just makes him all the more curious.

"You say that like I should be scared."

"Maybe you should be," I counter.

"You don't scare me," he teases.

"Oh, I don't? Are you sure about that?" I tease him back.

"Well, uh, not at the moment?" He's incredulous.

"That's what I thought." I unscrew the cap of my water and down it before recapping it and throwing it into the waste basket under the work table.

I turn back toward the bed and find Aryn's eyes are still on the bag, like he's trying to use x-ray vision to see through it. "There's a change of clothes in there," I tease.

"I doubt that's all."

"Why is that?" I ask.

"The way you're hunched over when you're carrying it."

I snort, "Well played." I gesture toward the bag. "Go ahead, open it."

With deliberately slow movements and shaking hands he reaches for the zipper. I don't intervene because there are some people who have to take the leap themselves.

I chuckle as his shaking fingers slide the zipper open and his shoulders slump in disappointment. "See, clothes," I tease

"You don't take an entire duffle bag, big enough for a girl to crawl into, full of clothes to the club," he says with a chuckle.

"If you're so sure about that, what do you think is in there?"

"Toys," he states simply.

I nod and smile. "You're right, move the clothes," I say with a commanding tone and his hands reach inside, grabbing the hangers the clothes are on.

My heart swells with pride when he doesn't look into the bag but rather takes the hangers of clothes over to the closet and hangs them up. "I take it that means you want me to stay?"

He pauses, lowering his head. "Yes, I do."

I sit down on the bed next to the bag of toys and I smirk. "Good, because I hadn't planned on leaving, not tonight anyway."

His face lights up with a wide smile as it spreads from ear to ear.

"Come, let's take a look. This might be another good way for you to decide what you may or may not like."

He nods with a little more enthusiasm as he comes back to the bed. He stands close to me, so close that my leg is touching his. There is a strange calmness that washes over me when our legs make contact. My heart skips a beat in my chest at the realization that his touch means something to me. It's calming me, comforting me.

I distract myself from my thoughts and say, "Go ahead take a look." And he does.

He opens the bag and his eyes go wide. I peer inside, seeing what he's seeing. Though rather unassuming to me, to him I imagine it's a bit overwhelming.

He lifts up what's sitting on top; six bunches of black silk rope. He scrutinizes them, questions forming in his eyes. "It's a great form of bondage," I tell him with a smirk, unable to hide the vision in my head of him tied up, completely at my mercy. There's no doubt the same vision swims through his mind when he shivers slightly before audibly swallowing hard. He gently sets the rope down on the bed.

Next comes the fun stuff. A couple of paddles that vary in length and width. His eyes go particularly wide at the thickest, widest one in there. Made of nicely polished wood to give it that added bit on impact. "It's heavy." His voice is sultry, filled with desire.

"It is and it hurts like a motherfucker," I chuckle humorlessly.

His eyes widen and he swallows hard again. "I don't think I like this one."

"You're not supposed to. That one, my boy, is more about punishment than pleasure. It packs a bite worse than skin to skin." I hold my hand up and wiggle my fingers. His eyes light up a little and narrow back to normal with that suggestion.

"I like that," he points to my hand with the paddle, "idea much better."

"So do I, sweet boy, so do I." I give him a mischievous smirk.

He sets the paddle down and reaches into the bag for one of the four floggers I carry in there. I smile as I stand up, taking it from his hand. His eyes go back toward the bag and he sees the others inside.

"There's a difference in how they feel. Can I show you?" I ask and he nods, unsure. I take a step back, rounding the foot of the bed. "Come over here and lean over with your hands on the bed," I tell him and he complies when I make room for him to do so. I go back to the foot of the bed and pull the other three floggers from inside the bag and lay them out on the bed for him to see.

"This one is heavy, so it's thuddy versus stingy," I explain as I stand behind him. My hard-on roars back with a vengeance as I look at Aryn's prone position. I swallow, trying to regain my composure

before I twirl the flogger a couple of times. "Relax, this is meant for education, not to hurt or harm you. All you need to do is say stop and I will do exactly that. Do you understand?"

"Yes, Master. I understand."

"Good."

Aryn

I have no idea what to expect.

Sure, Dex spent some time showing me some of what he has, but that was Dex using my arm with very little in the way of a physical connection between us. With Caden, I'm desperate to make this work. I have this compelling need to prove to Caden that this is what I want. I don't know why but I feel like everything between us right now is superficial. Like the thread could break at any moment. A shiver of insecurity slides through me.

My cock grew hard the moment I opened that bag and removed the clothes. Seeing everything he has in there is, well, there aren't any words for it. I just know by the throbbing in my jeans that I want this more than anything.

Caden's touch makes me jump when his hand slides up my back. His touch quickly calms me in a way I wasn't expecting. The warmth and softness causes my muscles to relax and my mind to give in. It lasts only a minute before his hand is gone. Before anxiety can worm its way into my brain, he flips the flogger and it lands against my back. "Ah," I breathe out.

"Do you like that, pet?" Caden says with a hint of approval in his voice. I nod my head.

He flips it again and it lands in almost the same spot, but he strikes

again before I can process the feeling of it. Each hit is a little harder than the previous and by the third one I can feel the little bites in my flesh caused by the ends of the falls.

Caden doesn't let up and I start to feel a very unfamiliar tingle radiating down my arms and legs. I close my eyes, shutting out everything but the sensation across my back. My head lulls downward as I relax into the motion of Caden's rhythmic flogging.

"More?" he asks. All I can manage is a mumble. "I can't hear you." His voice has altered, changed into something a little harder, edgier and it sends a new wave of desire through me.

"Yes," I say.

He stops. "Yes, what?"

My brain misfires, the disapproval in his tone sends a new wave of dread through me, it takes me a moment to realize what I've missed. "Please, Master?" I beg.

Silence falls on the room, a pin dropping on the floor right now would sound like a jar a marbles on a concrete floor. My breathing halts in my chest as fear that I've said something wrong slices through me.

My muscles tense. No doubt he can see it for himself.

His hand slides up my spine. The warmth of his palm comforts me. The silence in the room is broken by the whooshing sound the flogger makes as Caden begins spinning it, warming it up. There is no pain, no kiss of the flogger, only the growing fear of a punishing strike as his hand comes away from my back. The falls of the flogger are back, beating against me in quick succession. With each hit, the intensity grows and with each pass of the flogger over my skin, desire ignites like lava in my veins.

Caden doesn't stop. Each strike across my back sends blood racing through my veins, my breathing shallows and my mind goes blank. The tingling sensation radiating throughout my body is unlike anything I've ever felt before. It almost feels like fear, but I know

he will not hurt me. Gradually his strokes slow, each one hitting a little harder than the last. The slower pace gives me a moment to processes that there is no pain, only pleasure coursing through me.

It doesn't hurt, in fact, the harder he hits me, the foggier the world seems and the more aware of his presence I become. He's there, with me, guiding me under, taking me to a new world of heightened sensation I've never imagined before. My cock throbs harder in my jeans. The necessity to cum grows harder to control with each pass of the falls against my skin. Every nerve in my body is alive with sensation, a desperate need to be touched sings in my veins.

I let out a rush of breath I didn't know I was holding in on the next strike. This one hurts more than all the others have. I fight to pull air back into my lungs and relax. Before I can settle my tightened muscles, he strikes again. This one is more painful than the last one and I fight to regain control of my body, to relax myself. I realize that while painful, my cock throbs harder, my heart races faster, and my already foggy world grows foggier still. I settle into a rhythm of breathing and processing each stroke. Each time the world dips and comes back, dips and comes back to me.

He lightens his strokes and slows until he stops altogether.

Disappointment races like ice water in my veins.

*A*ryn's disappointment is evident. I could tell by the shallowness of his breathing and the trembling of his arms that he was slipping into a happy place. I try to calm his disappointment by sliding my hand along the slightly pink marks from the flogger. He arches his back into my touch and his breathing stutters. His back is warm with the rush of blood the flogging caused. It's a beautiful sight to see and feel. The warmth I feel is a tremendous comfort to me.

I put the flogger down on the bed and lean forward, sliding my hand farther up his back, along his neck and into his hair. I fist his hair and pull his head up as I come around the side of the bed so that I can look at him. His eyes are slow to open, his breathing ragged and shallow. My cock stirs in my jeans. His eyes slowly open. The desire I see in them sends a thrill through me.

Unable to resist showing my appreciation to him for a job well done, I slam my lips against his. He moans into my mouth as our lips begin moving in perfect harmony. I slide my tongue along his lower lip and he shivers. My already rock hard and swollen cock throbs as our tongues meet. A whimper escapes him as I claim his mouth.

His body and the bed start to shake as his arms begin losing their ability to hold him upright. With my free hand, I nudge his shoulder and we break the seal of our kiss. He stands up and I round the bed quickly. Taking his face between my palms I pull him in for another soul-crushing kiss. I press our bodies together. His erection presses against mine and we both groan.

I can barely breathe and his breaths come in short bursts.

I release him from our kiss, "well done, my sweet-sweet boy. Did you enjoy that?"

"Mm, yes Master," he says huskily.

I smile. "Good."

I claim his mouth once again.

His desperate hands begin tugging at my shirt and I put some distance between us, releasing his face from between my hands so that he can remove my shirt. An invitation he gladly accepts. When he's pulled my shirt over my head, breaking our kiss, he tosses it on to the bed. Then I slam my lips against his once more and let my hands roam over his naked chest, around his sides and up and down his back. Finally landing on the waistband of his jeans. Sliding my fingers around to the front. When I reach it, I don't hesitate to open the button and reach for the zipper. He doesn't stop me.

The zipper sticks and I break the kiss to look down. It takes me a second but I free the zipper and slide it all the way down, freeing my prize. I reach into his pants and with the lightest touch I can manage in my frenzied state I stroke my fingers along his cock. His eyes close, his body shivers and his breathing falters. I reach in a little farther and grab hold of his thick cock, pulling it free of its confinement. At the same time, I dip my head and flick my tongue across his nipple. He shudders and moans.

His breathing is erratic above me and my eyes meet his, barely open, as I lower myself to the floor on my knees. Without a word, I dart my tongue out, catching the swollen crest just enough to send another shiver through him and his eyes close as the pleasure skyrockets through him.

I lick again and he groans. "You do not have permission to come," I order him and his eyes go wide, locking with mine. I narrow mine slightly, conveying that what I say is the truth. "You can come only when I give you permission, do you understand?"

He nods his head slowly, though I can see the disappointment in his eyes as they return to their normal size.

"I want all your pleasure, Aryn, every single drop of it and I want you to willingly give it over to me."

"I don't know if I can." He takes a deep breath. "I'll do my best, Master."

40

I give him a satisfied grin. "That is all I'm asking for."

He nods again as I flick my tongue across the tip of his swollen cock. His eyes flutter closed with pleasure as I hook my thumbs in the waistband of his jeans and pull them down until I reach his knees. Trapping him. A satisfied smirk plays on my lips as I glide my hands up his thighs toward his hips until sliding them around to grab hold of his tight, gorgeous ass cheeks. I pull his body toward mine. His cock slides farther down my throat and I look up at him. Watching him closely, I pull back slightly, flicking my tongue along his shaft. His muscles tense and his eyes scrunch closed. I suck him back into my mouth, straight to the back of my throat. I swallow, his cock twitches and I'm treated to a little burst of pre-cum. His taste, his smell, the overwhelming need to have him quickly consumes me and rattles my control.

Fighting for a distraction, I loosen my grip and let my hands roam along his backside and down, spreading his cheeks wide. When my finger glides along his tight entrance his mouth falls slack and a breathy moan escapes his lips and I shiver. I let his cock slide from my mouth with a smile of approval on my face when his eyes find mine. I wrap my lips around the head of his cock once again and gently suck him down. At the same time I swirl my finger along the rim of his tight hole and his eyes roll up in his head. His body is trembling above me, teetering close to falling over. His ability to stand is fading fast and the image of Aryn tied to a cross sends a new wave of pleasure through me as my already hard cock stretches further behind my jeans.

I can't stop now. I don't want to stop. His cock fills my mouth with such delicious pre-cum and my mind fills with all sorts of ideas that drive me crazy.

I let his cock slide in and out of my mouth while my finger gently rubs along his back entrance. I move my free hand to take his cock so I can pump and suck on him as my finger continues to press into him gently. I stretch my hand a little, giving my thumb access to

that sensitive spot just below his sack and I stroke softly. So many sensations at once has got to be making my command to not come very difficult. But he's doing it and I admire him a little more for it.

After a few more passes, I can tell he's about to lose it. His cock is rigid, hard as steel. His head swells in my mouth.

"Ahh," he cries out, his body swaying. "I can't...I'm gonna..." I pull back my fingers and slowly release his cock with an audible pop and I look up at him. It takes him a moment to open his eyes and look down at me. When he does, his lids are heavy with desire and I'm ready to take this to the next level.

I stand, cupping the back of his neck before pulling him toward my lips. I press our lips together in a fervent, desperate kiss. I'm finding it harder to control myself with each passing breath between us. I move my tongue along his, consuming him and letting my mind wander to the idea of him kneeling before me.

Pulling back from our kiss, I look at his swollen lips. Knowing I did that to him sends a thrill of desire through my veins and I grab hold of his cock once again. The moment my fingers make contact, his eyes roll back and his already ragged breathing hitches in his throat. Seeing the pleasure on his face sends me reaching for the button of my jeans with my free hand. I quickly unbutton them and slide the zipper down, freeing my cock.

The cool air of the room swirls around my heated erection causing me to shiver. I need to feel what he's feeling so I take his hand in mine, guiding it toward my erection. His eyes slowly open, curious about what I plan to do. His eyes widen briefly when I place his hand on my cock. The surprise in his eyes fades fast when the warmth of his hand pulls me under. My eyes flutter and my control waivers. Pleasure sparks need. Need to come, need to feel his mouth on me, a need to feel myself inside him, claiming him. My mouth falls slack as he strokes again and again. I release his cock, giving him room to move and without instruction, he lowers himself to his knees.

With my cock still in his hand, he strokes it a couple times before

running my tip over his lips. He's torturing me in ways I haven't experience in a long time. I fight the urge to pull my Dom stare. Forcing him to do this isn't what I want to do and there is a good possibility that if I push this too far, too fast, he'll pull away from me. I'm no stranger to another man, but he is and I want to respect that and him.

After a few torturous heartbeats, he opens his mouth. His tongue darts out and licks along the head of my cock. Pleasure explodes. I slide my hand into his hair, not to guide him, but to show him that I'm here with him, that I'm in this too. I can't pull my eyes away from where his look up at me. Seeing my approval, he leans in closer and swipes his tongue from base to tip before flicking quickly against the underside of the head. I tremble with need. "That's it, my sweet boy."

My tone gives him all the approval he needs and he takes the next step when he wraps his swollen lips around the head of my cock. His eyes are still focused on me but the pleasure is too much to handle and I can't stop my eyes from closing as the sensation overwhelms me. To show him some more encouragement, I squeeze my hand in his hair, tugging slightly, and he moans around my cock. The vibration sends a new wave of lust through me.

With my hand in his hair, I encourage him by pulling him toward me. I want to feel my cock in his mouth and I get the feeling he needs to know that's what I want.

We've not really established any rules, for him or for me, which means I am trying to let this fall into the casual category, for his sake and my own.

He sucks my cock farther into his mouth until I feel the back of his throat. His body stiffens slightly and I realize he's not breathing. I loosen my grip in his hair and what sounds like a whimper escapes him. Testing him, I tighten my hand again. He moans once again before pulling himself back and releasing my cock completely. He pulls in a deep breath and looks up at me. I cock my head at him. "Again?" I ask and he nods before taking my length back inside his mouth.

I can't help guiding him along my cock and it's an unbelievable feeling having my dick buried in his mouth. He sucks me all the way; once again cutting off his oxygen, this time for a shorter period of time, and when he pulls back, my cock is covered in a thick coating of saliva.

Seeing an opportunity to help this along, he wraps his warm hand around my cock, stroking a couple of times before he puts his lips on me again. He strokes up and down in time with his mouth. Watching him is a beautiful sight. His prone position, his cock bouncing with his motions, and my raging hard-on has me close to losing control as he consumes me.

My release is closer than I want it to be, and from his fervent pumping and sucking, he's trying to make me come. I slide my other hand into his hair, gripping the strands tightly. He moans again, this time louder, more intense. I start to thrust my hips gently, pushing my cock into his mouth, silently telling him to go faster. He relaxes beneath me. His jaw goes slack. His eyes meet mine and there is a look that steals the breath from my lungs. The look of lust, desire and most dominant of all, adoration.

Allowing me more access, he drops his hand, giving me full use of his mouth and I take the opportunity to slide my cock in and out of his mouth a little harder, a little deeper and a little faster. Without any guidance from me, his hand comes up to cup my balls, rolling them between his fingers. It's nearly enough to send me over the edge and into a spectacular orgasm and while I want to explode down his throat, but this wasn't exactly how I'd imagined my orgasm tonight.

I allow him to take to me to the point of explosion and I pull out of his mouth. He whimpers at me, his eyes full of sadness. He knows I was close. I fight for a few deep breaths to help find my center, to take back control of my body and most importantly, my cock. Slowly my pending orgasm subsides, though my need to come rages on like wildfire.

I let that desperation fuel me. "Take off your clothes and climb on the bed, now," I order and despite being confused by my abrupt halt and command, he stands, kicking off his shoes and sliding his pants from his legs before climbing on the bed. He crawls across the bed and I get a gorgeous view of his ass. Perfect.

While he settles, I pick up the stuff from the bag, tossing it back inside and zipping it closed. There are condoms in there and I fight the urge to grab one. The need to claim him as mine is roaring almost as powerful as my need to come. But I can't, not tonight. When I claim him, I want to claim him the right way, the way he deserves and I hardly qualify our first time together as the right time.

Then again, if I were any kind of a gentleman at all, we wouldn't be naked right now.

He settles on the bed, on his side, facing me, watching me. He doesn't say anything but looking at his naked body spread out on the bed is beyond anything I could have imagined. He's so sexy and sure and yet there is a gorgeous hint of the submission he's offering me. The comfort and pride I take in that is more than any other submissive I've ever had at my disposal. None of them hold a candle in comparison to Aryn, not just physically, but how I feel emotionally about this newfound relationship that's building between us.

CHAPTER NINE

Aryn

*C*oming without permission? What kind of torture is this? I get it, I do, but Jesus, it's killing me. I've nearly lost it so many times. But every time I think about coming, I remember what I told myself over and over again before entering the club. It's no longer about me, it's about him and about pleasing him, and if that means being tortured to the point of painful blue-balls, I'll do it. There is definitely one thing to be said about the desire to please and the unwillingness to disappoint, it's enough to make your orgasm disappear completely.

Lying down on the bed as Caden puts away the stuff we took out of the bag earlier, I think back to him flogging me. I cannot wait to do that again, and I'm beyond curious to feel what it will be like when he's not holding back. When he's going beyond just showing me what it feels like. The thought sends a shiver through my veins as he puts the flogger back in the bag. I never could have imagined something so intimidating could be so pleasurable. I didn't think I had it in me to truly hand myself over to the mercy of another human being. To put my life, my safety and most of all, my control, into someone else's hands wasn't something I expected to come so naturally. What Caden did to me tonight just proves further that I've made the right decision in being his submissive. Whether it's only temporary and I decide that being a Top is more important to me, or permanent, I don't know yet. I just want to enjoy the moment. I'll think about tomorrow, tomorrow.

Caden's eyes roam over my naked body laid out on the bed, waiting impatiently for what's going to happen next. I know what I want to happen, but I also know that this isn't necessarily about what I want. It's about pleasing Caden and further proving my willingness and desire to submit to him.

He stumbles awkwardly as he kicks off his shoes and then finally his jeans and I am now looking at a naked, tattoo-covered Caden as he stands at the foot of my bed. His cock is hard as a rock and

bounces with each little movement, making my mouth water. I can't help the quick dart of my tongue along my lips and I'm sure my eyes are giving away my hunger. He smirks as he takes his cock in his hand and he strokes it gently. The pleasure is obvious in the straining veins of his biceps as he attempts to control himself and my own cock twitches in anticipation.

"See something you like?" His voice is sultry and that subtle hint of command is there.

"Yes, Master," I tell him with a whisper.

"What would that be, boy?"

"Your cock in my mouth, Master."

"I like the sound of that," he murmurs as he steps to his left, toward the head of the bed. I start to roll onto my stomach, to put myself in a position to take his cock into my mouth. He pins me with a hard stare that sends ice into my veins so I stop and go back to laying on my side.

I've managed to confuse myself a few times tonight but the ease in which I am responding to him and his commands confirms my desire to submit. I'm enjoying it immensely but it doesn't stop me from analyzing the fact that he has this kind of hold on me. A part of me feels like I'm losing control of my own body. I'm handing the reigns to him and it's heady and a little uncomfortable.

I pout at him.

He chuckles as he climbs on to the bed and lays down, his head lining up with my cock. His cock is just inches from my waiting mouth and I lick my lips again. He slides in closer, wrapping an arm around my hips as he does, pulling me into him and bringing his cock to my mouth.

I catch on to what it is he's trying to do and I want to do the same with him, but a part of me is afraid to touch him without permission. I don't know if it's allowed. We haven't discussed it and everything I've done tonight so far has been at his urging.

"Are you waiting for permission?" His voice is gentle, approving.

I nod my head before realizing he really can't see me so I answer softly, "Yes, Master, I am."

"Take it, Aryn, take it and suck it."

I groan and wrap my arm around his hips, pulling him in close and I open my mouth, sucking him down hard and fast. "Ahh, fuck," he groans before sucking my cock deep into his own mouth. I moan around his cock and I'm rewarded with a tiny taste of what I hope is about to come for me. He stops sucking briefly. "Don't stop, Aryn," he murmurs and I don't. I suck him in fast and hard, bobbing my head along his cock. He immediately returns to sucking me in a similar fashion.

His little grunts and moans around my cock vibrate down into my balls and deeper into me, driving my need to orgasm higher. In an attempt at stopping myself from exploding down his throat, I concentrate on what I'm doing to him. Focusing my attention on giving him pleasure and not on the pleasure he's equally desperate to give me. Remembering earlier when I was stroking and sucking him, I try and grab a hold of his cock. It's difficult in this position, but I do what I can.

The hand he wrapped around my hips moves and I feel his gentle touch roaming along the swell of my cheeks before finding my entrance again.

I've had my hole played with before but never like what he does and when he makes contact, I feel my cock jump in his mouth. I rub my hand along his back, encouraging him to keep going. He does, but he also shifts his position enough so that he can open his legs. He's opening himself up to me and I'm momentarily surprised as I realize he wants me to do the same to him as he's doing to me. I smile around the head of his cock before sucking it in, hard and deep as I press a finger against his entrance.

My finger makes contact and he groans around my cock. All the angst and worry I had about taking this step fades quickly. He presses

his finger into me, sucking my cock deeper into his mouth and my ability to concentrate and distract myself disappears completely. Realizing that I am still desperate to please and pleasure him and I don't have permission to come pushes me to focus once again.

I flick my tongue along his shaft, working my way up to the head and manage to swirl my finger around his entrance and he pushes a little further into mine. I release his cock as I cry out as pleasure explodes. "I can't. Hold. It," I grunt out, but he doesn't stop. He thrusts his hips at me, his cock catching my cheek and I open my mouth, focusing hard on what I need to do. I can barely concentrate.

My orgasm roars with vengeance as Caden's finger slides gently in and out of me, though it's barely the tip. It doesn't matter, it's sending waves of pleasure and a desperate need to come exploding through my body and I lock down as my orgasm becomes too much for me to handle any more. I suck hard on his cock and he pushes his hips forward and pulls them back, fucking my mouth and I let him.

I feel cool air consume my cock. "Come for me, my gorgeous pet. Come for me now," he orders before he sucks my cock back into his mouth, swallowing as much of me as he is able. His finger presses harder and deeper into me and I explode down his throat. My orgasm vibrates through my lips and into his cock as he thrusts in short bursts into my mouth. I press into his entrance and am rewarded with his moans of pleasure as he shoots down my throat. I fight to swallow everything down as he is doing the same. His finger has moved and it's only the sensation of his mouth on me that wrings out the rest of my orgasm and I milk his cock for every drop he has to give me.

I slowly pull myself off his cock and while he's no longer sucking mine, it doesn't stop him from teasing me by licking the underside, the sensitive part that makes me jump with each little flick of his tongue. I groan as I roll half onto my back, unable to keep myself on my side any longer and Caden does the same. But his hand comes to rest on top of my chest. No doubt he can feel my heart pounding

beneath the surface and I'm not sure who needs the contact more, him or me.

My cock is still semi-hard and I look over at his. We're both in the same uncomfortable boat, but I know that if I stop thinking about it, I'll soften. Eventually.

We don't say anything for some time. We just lie there as our breathing returns to normal and my heartbeat slows to a nice relaxed pace.

Caden moves, sitting up and sliding toward the end of the bed. For some reason, I feel like he's going to leave and I really don't want that to happen.

"Shower with me?" he asks and I look up at him. There's a gentle, playful smile on his face and I can't stop myself from rolling over and off the bed to join him.

He leads me into the bathroom where he turns on the rainfall shower and sets the temperature before taking my hand and ushering me inside.

CHAPTER TEN

Showering with anyone is a novelty I've never experienced before. When you're constantly taking women in the backs of bars, cars and the occasional hotel room, it's hard to actually do things like this. Then again, you have to want to do things like this and up until right now, I've never wanted to. It's an odd feeling, letting someone pamper me. Isn't this what I should be doing to him or to a woman? Why does he feel the need to do it for me? I can tell this is going to take some getting used to and I'm going to have to figure it out, quick. Showering with Caden is a novelty I've never experienced before.

Caden takes his time. I feel oddly cherished when he washes me from neck to feet. I worried that I would feel emasculated by being taken care of, but I don't. In an attempt to please him, I try to return the favor, but he stops me. "This is about me taking care of you," he says with a tone that screams 'don't argue with me, you will lose', so I don't.

When he gets to my cock, which has grown hard as a rock again, he lathers his hands up and pays special attention to it as he strokes me with both of his hands, one hand slipping down to fondle my sack. I fight to keep myself upright by placing a hand on the wall of the shower. God, I don't want him to stop, but I get the impression that he will, but he doesn't.

I look down at our two bodies close together and his cock is growing hard between us. I reach for him, wanting to return the favor and the pleasure, but he pulls back, out of my reach. I pout at him. I reach for it but he pulls back from me, pulling it out of reach again and I pout.

He releases my cock, bringing one of his hands to his lips as if he is pondering something. "I have to admit, you pouting is a nice touch," he smirks, "but it will never work on me."

The hand he'd brought to his lips comes down and wraps around my forearm. His free hand does the same thing. The next thing I know, my hands are being raised over my head and I'm being pressed against the cool tile wall. I hiss through my teeth as the cold tile registers in my brain. Caden gives me a satisfied smirk.

I'm effectively trapped between the wall's unrelenting surface and Caden's rock hard body. With the water now cascading over him, he slams his lips against mine as he presses me to the wall, making it impossible for me to move. I feel his knee pressing between my thighs, wanting me to spread for him and I don't hesitate to do so.

His leg slides between my legs, forcing me to give him room. He slides his leg up, pressing it again my sack. It's almost painful, but he's immobilized me completely. Our cocks are pressed against each other in between our bodies. He thrust his hips upwards forcing our cocks to rub together. My eyes roll as the pleasure skyrockets through my system.

He adjusts himself so that both of my arms are pinned in one of his hands before bringing his free hand down my arm gently. I squirm because it tickles and he smiles against my lips. His hand continues down my side and again I squirm and laugh a little. I open my eyes to see his looking at me with pleasure and approval. He pulls back from our kiss, giving us a little space to allow our breathing to return to normal. I suck in a deep breath through my teeth when his free hand wraps around both our cocks and he pulls up, stroking both our cocks at the same time.

I'm pinned.

I'm immobilized.

I'm at his mercy.

My orgasm races quickly to the surface. I slam my eyes shut, fighting off the rage of emotions as I feel the need to come rocketing through me again. This time it's unrelenting.

Caden's teeth nip at my lip, then kisses and little nips along my

jaw, then down my neck as he holds me tight to the wall. His hand continues stoking along our shafts and I bite my lip, praying for the strength to hold in my orgasm until I realize that he hasn't denied me an orgasm. He hasn't told me that I can't come.

"Oh god," I cry out. "No, no, no..."

"No, what?"

I pull in a deep breath. "I...you didn't give me permission, but you didn't...ahh," I groan as he strokes harder against our cocks. "You didn't tell me I had to ask. I...ahh," I cry out again.

"You want to come, pet?"

"Yes, Master...but I..." My breathing is nearly nonexistent and I open and close my eyes, fighting to retain control of my desperate need to come. "You didn't give me permission."

"No, and you haven't asked, my pet"

"Oh god." He strokes again, his knee raising up a little higher, pressing into my balls and there is a sharp twinge of pain, but rather than sending ice through my veins, it ignites the fire hotter, brighter than it was just a moment ago. "Please?" I beg.

"Please what?" he growls in my ear as he strokes up and pushes down on our cocks.

"Please, Master, please," I beg.

His hand strokes harder, faster.

"Please, Master, please I need to come."

"You're still not asking me anything, pet."

"I know... Ahhh." The pain of his knee is nothing compared to the pain I'm starting to feel as I fend off my raging orgasm. I don't know how I'm doing it, but I am. Disappointing him is not something I can do, not here, not tonight and not ever. "Please Master, please may I come?" I finally manage to get it all out through gritted teeth.

Fear slices through me, throwing down the ice I needed a minute ago when he doesn't answer me right away, but I'm brought right

back to the brink when he strokes again and again along our cocks.

I open my eyes. He's looking at me but he too is highly unfocused and I realize he's standing on the edge of the same cliff I am and on a bold move, I lean in and press my lips to his. His mouth consumes mine in a heartbeat and he pulls back. "Now, you may come." He pushes into me, pressing his lips to mine and his hand moves faster. My orgasm explodes out of my body. My cum mixes with his as his orgasm rocks through him at the same time. My knees weaken, trembling, causing me to relax which puts more pressure on my balls. The pain is so intense that it instantly pushes me over the edge of another orgasm.

"Oh fuck...fuck, fuck," I cry out.

Caden pulls back, still holding my hands, but he moves his leg and my knees nearly give out as he releases his cock and just takes mine as he milks out my third unexpected orgasm. Fear of him being upset settles over me like oil and I look at him with fear and worry raging between my ears. My heart squeezes when I see a look on his face I can't read while he slows pulling my shaft.

As soon as he's satisfied, he removes his hand from my shaft. He grips my arms and lowers them down the wall. My body burns with the strain of exhaustion, like I've run a marathon. He gently presses his body against mine, holding me against the wall, holding me up so I don't collapse onto the tile floor. I'm not sure what has me weak, the exhaustion of the night or the unwelcome rush of fear coursing through my veins.

Having him close to me is another unexpected need. I don't want him to leave me here, so in an attempt to keep him in place I grab hold of hips before I can manage my apology. "I'm sorry, Master," I finally breathe.

"What are you sorry for, my dear sweet boy?" He cocks his head in confusion.

"I didn't have permission," I whisper.

He pulls back so I can see his face. "For a spontaneous second orgasm?" He narrows his eyes in question.

I just nod my head. I can't say anything else, unsure of how to read him.

"Tell me something?"

"Anything, Master," I breathe.

"What set it off?" His voice is full of curiosity and I can't not tell him.

"When I came, I slipped, crushing my sack against your leg."

His eyes light up and his lips twitch with a knowing smile. "So, pain gets you off." He states this as a fact and not as a question.

I ponder his statement a moment and he checks that I'm steady before letting me stand on my own.

"I guess it does, but I," I shake my head, "I've been in excruciating pain before and, oh god," I breathe as I realize that I cannot honestly tell this man it didn't turn me on.

"You got hard?"

"Not exactly, considering I'd been clipped in the nuts with a boot." I can see the wheels turning with the light in his eyes. "That is something I never, ever want to experience again and that is a very hard limit." I narrow my eyes and continue, "But eventually it did. After I got over being pissed being kicked and the initial pain settled a bit, I got hard. Anytime I had a wave a pain roll through, I would get hard." I can feel the heat rising in my cheeks as I share. "Anytime I was hurt and had a chance to recover a bit, when the residual pain would hit, I'd get hard."

By the time I'm done telling him all this, he's all but bouncing with excitement. "So, about that whip?" he teases me and once again, pleasure and desire rocket through me. Though I don't get hard from the idea, my balls tingle with anticipation. "That's what I thought."

"In time, please Caden, I can't just..."

"What did you call me?"

Disappointment slices through me. "I'm sorry. Master."

He gives me a playful smile as he presses into me gently, his lips mere inches from mine. "I like it when you call me Caden," he admits before gently pressing his lips against mine one more time.

CHAPTER ELEVEN

I dry Aryn off and then myself before we return to the bedroom. Aryn is exhausted. His eyes are heavy and his movements are lethargic, either that or I am that tired. I turn down the sheets on the bed and ask, "Do you have a side?"

"Odd question?" He quirks an eyebrow at me.

"I, uh, it's your bed, regardless."

He huffs a small laugh. "I sleep in the middle."

"Good," I tell him with a smirk and I gesture for him to come to me. I'm not giving him a chance to put anything on and he doesn't seem to mind when he steps up to me. "Climb in," I tell him, and though there isn't any command in my voice he does so without hesitation and he slides to the middle, adjusting the pillows as he does. He rolls to his right side, facing away from me and my smirk grows into a wider smile after I turn the light off and climb in behind him.

I wrap my arm around him, spreading my fingers along his stomach and I settle in behind him after snaking my arm up under his pillow.

"You comfortable?" I ask.

"Mm, very." He wiggles his hips and I feel his butt rubbing along my cock. The hand that was holding him comes away and I smack his ass, pretty hard, but not enough to really hurt him.

"Oww," he squeaks then laughs. I return my hand to his stomach and I kiss him on the shoulder.

"Sleep, my sweet boy."

"Good night."

I jolt awake.

Blinking wildly, breathing hard.

I fight to remember where I am and then it comes back to me in a wild rush.

The club.

Ashley...Dex, the secret, Aryn coming to the club, and eventually ending up here, his hotel room. Unable to tell the time inside the pitch dark room, my head lulls toward the clock on the nightstand. It's three forty-five in the morning. I climbed into bed an hour ago and fell asleep to the soft snores coming from Aryn as he slept. At some point I'd managed to pull myself away from him, though I don't remember doing it and I strain to see him in the darkness. I can't see him but the steady rhythm of his breathing is enough for me to know he's there.

I stare blankly up at the ceiling that I can't really see until my eyes adjust to the lack of light.

I knew sleeping in the same bed wasn't going to be easy for me. I've never done it. Well, at least not with a submissive. The last person I slept in the same bed with was Shelly and that was a very long time ago.

I scrub my face.

My mind wanders back to what woke me in the first place. A dream, a Shelly dream, a dream I haven't had in years. But the end result is always the same. No matter how many times I try to take a different road; the end result is always exactly what it is.

Only this time, she talked to me. "I only ever wanted you to be happy," she'd murmured right before it happened.

I rub my hand along my left side, the dull ache is back.

Not wanting to disturb Aryn, I climb out of bed and go into the bathroom. I close the door and turn the light on, catching a glimpse of my disheveled self in the mirror. I turn the water on and wash my face with cold water. Trying to clear my head of all things Shelly, but I fail when I fall back into a nearly long forgotten memory of us in a hotel similar to this one.

I'd been on set all day. She'd come to the location for the weekend, but we were running over so she'd come to the lot. She'd watched me work for quite a while. Then the rain hit and of course it was freezing cold.

I shudder at the memory and it comes back to me in full swing.

"Go inside, Shell-belle, I don't want you getting sick."

"But I like watching you work."

I laugh a little at that one and she gives me her super pouty face. "Alright, we're almost done anyway," I tell her and kiss her quickly before returning to one of the cameras to watch the action sequence playing out before me.

When it doesn't go right, I call cut and go into the middle of their fighting and we play it out again, one more time. They'd better get this or I'm gonna lose my shit.

I just want to get Shelly back to the hotel and warm her up. I haven't seen my girl in more than three weeks and I miss her like crazy.

"Get it right, you guys. You know this."

"What crawled up your ass?" one of my stunt doubles asks me.

"Forget it. Let's just get it done so we can get the fuck out of here, please?"

"Yeah, alright."

They didn't get it on that take. After more than two hours and countless takes, the scene was finally captured the right way.

As soon as I am clear, Shelly and I bolt back to the hotel.

She's a frozen mess by the time we get to our room. We hop into a hot shower together.

God, I can't keep my hands off her, but I'm finished before her so I get out and dry off. I'm standing in front of the mirror when she comes up behind me, unraveling my towel while she kisses my shoulder...

I close my eyes.

I can still see her beautiful face smiling back at me in the mirror.

I haven't lost this much control on my thoughts about Shelly in a very, very long time. I never needed to. In reality, I've never felt even remotely close to what I feel for Shelly toward anyone else. While I'm not entirely certain I feel that way toward Aryn, he's definitely come the closest and that is unsettling.

She was my life, my everything.

I splash some more cold water on my face before toweling off and heading back into the bedroom. I leave the bathroom light on but close the door to just a crack behind me. The faint light illuminates enough of the room that I can find my pants at the foot of the bed and I go digging for my cell. I find it and pull it out of my pocket before making myself comfortable in the chair under the window.

I power it on and wait while several emails and a couple of text messages silently come over the phone.

I have texts from Derek and Ashley.

I open Ashley's first.

Ash to Caden: I didn't see you guys leave, hope all is well.

I don't text her back for two reasons. One, it's four in the morning and two, she's fishing for information and I'm not about to give it to her.

I open Derek's message next.

Derek to Caden: I honestly had no clue about tonight, but I'm glad. Haven't seen you so happy in a long time. Dex and Raine are here till Tuesday, dinner Monday night?

If Dex and Raine are leaving on Tuesday that means Aryn isn't far behind. Crap, that really sucks.

I text Derek back, despite the hour, his phone is silent.

> Caden to Derek: I know you didn't, it's all good. Great surprise, but it kept me off kilter most of the night. Can't sleep. I'll discuss with A about Monday.

Derek, like me, is often up long before the sun comes up and this morning is no exception.

> Derek to Caden: Aryn not going home with D/R, at least not that I know of. Off kilter is a good thing, means he'll keep you on your toes. Let me know. Teddy said you're having lunch there today. Let me know if you free up this evening.
> Caden to Derek: Can do, thanks my friend.

Derek doesn't reply, didn't expect him to.

I scrub my hand over my hair, exhausted. Aryn stirs on the bed, rolling over and I hear what sounds like a hand in the sheets, searching. I look at him as he sits up to look for me.

"Hey," he says with a sleep laced voice. "You okay?"

I frown. "Just can't sleep."

"Come back to bed?" he asks.

"In a few minutes, I didn't mean to wake you."

He scrubs his face with his free hand. "You didn't."

I nod with a sad smile and he lies back down. It takes but a few heartbeats before his gentle snoring returns, soft and even.

"**W**ake up, sleepy head."

"Mmhmm," Aryn groans.

"Come on, we gotta get going."

"Hmm?" His eyes open and meet mine.

"Lunch, remember?"

"Oh." He rubs at his eyes as he tries to wake up. "Did you sleep?"

"A little."

"I hate to ask it, but did I do something?"

I gently stroke his cheek. "No, not at all. It's just not something I'm used to."

"Sleeping?" He quirks an eyebrow at me.

I chuckle a little at his expression. "No, sleeping next to someone."

"Oh." I can see the wheels turning as he fights for a follow-up question.

"It's been ten years since I've slept next to anyone," I tell him and I know he's going to ask questions about why that is and I plan to tell him, just not now and not today.

His eyes go wide briefly before they narrow in speculation. "Not even with any of your subs?"

"No, my submissive relationships have been limited to the club environment, for lack of a shorter explanation. I'm not in the habit of dating my submissives, Aryn. We've talked about this."

"So, is that all you want from me? Just to submit to you and that's it? Nothing more?"

I sit back on the bed. "No, it's not what I want anymore."

"That's cryptic," he mumbles.

"I mean, yes, I want you as my submissive." I scrub at my face.

"I don't know how to do anything else," I tell him honestly and it's true.

"I'm not asking you to throw everything you have into this, Caden. I simply would like an open mind, for both of us, to consider that this might actually be more than a D/s relationship."

I give him a small smile. "My mind is open, I assure you."

"Good," he says before propping himself up on his elbow and taking my hand in his. "I'd kiss you, but morning breath like this shouldn't be exposed to anyone." He laughs, squeezes my hand and climbs off the bed on the opposite side and he heads for the bathroom. I watch him go, admiring that gorgeous ass of his until it's out of sight.

He doesn't close the door all the way when he goes in there and I wait until I hear the water running before I get off the bed and follow him in there.

I push open the door and lean into the frame as I watch him wash his face then grab his toothbrush. He gives me a sideways smirk as he puts toothpaste on the bristles and then into his mouth.

"Who knew that teeth brushing could be so sexy?" he chuckles as he starts brushing his teeth and I step up behind him and wrap my hands around him.

His eyes meet mine in the mirror and there is a playful smile on his lips as I kiss his shoulder. I let one of my hands slide down the ridges of his abdomen. He watches my hand disappear below the counter in the mirror and I grab ahold of his cock. Already hard. He stops brushing and his eyes roll up as I stroke his cock. "Keep brushing. I need those lips," I breathe and he feverishly brushes his teeth while I stroke his cock in a slow, torturous up and down pace.

He leans over and spits out his toothpaste before grabbing a glass and filling it up, all while his hands are trembling and my hand hasn't stopped moving.

"You keep that up and I'm going to come all over the counter." He smiles playfully at me. A new novelty to me - letting someone dictate what I'm doing, but I'm not feeling very dominant this morning so I let it go, biting gently on his shoulder as he spits the water from his mouth.

He stands up straight and turns his head toward me. I press my lips to his.

He moans into my mouth and I slide my tongue along his peppermint flavored tongue.

After a few more beats, I pull back, releasing his lips from mine and pulling my hand away from his cock. He visibly pouts. "Later, my pet. We've got to get going, remember?"

He frowns and nods.

"Oh believe me; I will make it worth the wait." I kiss his shoulder once again and walk from the bathroom.

My own raging erection strains against my boxer briefs.

When Aryn comes into the room he looks at the clock on the night stand. "It's barely ten in the morning. I thought lunch was at one?"

"It is, but I'd like to ask you to check out today and come stay at my house until you leave."

"Which you still don't want to know when that is?"

I shake my head. "No, I don't want to put a time limit on the length of your stay. Though I do know Dex and Raine are leaving on Tuesday and as far as Derek knows, you're not going back with them?" I cock my head,

"I'd hoped to not be going back with them."

I smile. "Good, so will you check out of here and come stay with me?"

"Absolutely."

"Now pack," I smirk and he smiles wide before going for his suitcase in the closet.

I'm rewarded with a naked show as he hasn't gotten dressed yet.

Forty minutes of naked packing later I say, "Not that I mind the view, but were you planning on getting dressed?"

He laughs, "Yeah, I guess I should do that."

"Well, it's pretty cold outside, you might be more comfortable," I chuckle and he pulls out a pair of jeans and one of his black t-shirts. I'm disappointed that he's covering up.

Another hour later and we're pulling up in front of Teddy's house. Aryn's luggage is in the back of my SUV. "A few rules," I tell him as we sit there. His eyes are wide as he takes in the size of Teddy's home and I am reminded once again that this isn't a norm for him. I worry about how he's going to feel about my house when we get there later tonight. "Teddy and Will live a twenty-four/seven lifestyle. Will has more liberties at home and it's rather informal, but I do expect you to address Teddy as sir. I'm not ever going to ask you to remain quiet and you have permission from me as well as Teddy to freely talk to Will or anyone for that matter."

"So, it's like being around normal friends?" he asks.

"It is. With the exception of Teddy and addressing him as sir. He, after all, is still a Top and no submissive should forget that."

"And you?"

I smile wide at him. "Caden is fine." I take his hand in mine and squeeze it. "I like it."

He smiles at me and nods before we climb out of the car.

Will is standing in the doorway as we approach. "Hello, Sir, Aryn."

"Hi Will, spying again?" I chuckle. I can see the visible panic in Will.

"No, Sir, I just heard your doors close."

I chuckle, "You're good, Will."

"Oh, thank god." He visibly relaxes as he ushers us inside. "Teddy is in the kitchen," he tells me and I lead the three of us toward the back of the house where the kitchen is.

Realization dawns quickly. I may have no choice but to have that conversation with Aryn sooner than I'd planned. We step into A picture lined hallway. The pictures range from Teddy and Shelly's childhood, then into college with a ton of pictures of Teddy, Shelly and me, up to current pictures of Teddy and Will. Among those pictures are pictures of Teddy, Will and I, sans Shelly. Fuck.

Aryn

Caden ushers the two of us through the house and my eyes land on the walls filled with pictures. Of course, I recognize Teddy and Will, but I'm surprised to see Caden in so many pictures with Teddy and even with Will. There is a woman who repeats through most of the pictures and I have no idea who she is, but she's gorgeous. She's got lengthy blonde hair that's wavy in a way that looks natural. Her beauty isn't from a bottle. She wears very little makeup and her eyes are bright and they look to be the same as Teddy's. A family resemblance?

I don't stop following Caden so, I can't take a real good look at all of them but I make plans to do so at some point while we're here. The pictures morph into more of Teddy and Will the closer we get to the kitchen that I see ahead of us.

Caden enters first, then myself and finally, Will.

"Hey," Teddy says to Caden and they exchange knowing looks and there's an air of panic on Caden's face which Teddy reads quickly. "Hey, Aryn," Teddy says to me.

"Hello, sir." He smiles at my address.

"Will, why don't you give Aryn a tour of the house. Lunch is still another thirty minutes from being done."

"Yes, Daddy," Will says and he grabs my arm, pulling me back into the hallway, but he doesn't slow down long enough for me to look.

Caden

"What's wrong?" Teddy asks me as soon as the boys leave the room.

I shake my head. "I'd forgotten about the walls." I nod in the direction the boys just went.

Teddy shrugs, "What about it?"

"Shell?"

"You haven't told him?" Teddy slides a bottle of water across the kitchen island toward me.

"No, I've hardly had the chance to do so, and I certainly didn't want to spoil the night we were having." I sigh as I unscrew the cap on the bottle and take a swallow. "I was hoping to avoid it longer."

Teddy frowns at me. "Keeping him in the dark isn't an option if you want this to work."

"I know, it's just," I close my eyes, "I'm not ready. Aryn as my sub I'm prepared for, but cracking those walls..." I shake my head, I feel so deflated and Teddy knows it.

"You can always shut him down."

I shake my head. "No, I can't. I opened the can this morning."

"He didn't see the pictures at your house?" he asks.

I shake my head. "No, we went back to his hotel room last night."

Teddy frowns at me. "Then how did you open the can?"

"I slept next to him for about an hour before I bolted awake. I've been up since three or four." I scrub at my face. "I didn't even know I'd dozed off until I bolted awake. The dream came back," I tell him and he knows what I'm talking about without elaboration. "Only it was different. Right before it happened she said that she only ever wanted me to be happy."

"You have to believe that's true, Caden."

"I do, it's just, I didn't expect it to be thrown in my face in a dream while I was sleeping next to the first person since her."

"She has a way of doing that," he tells me dismissively while he goes back to preparing lunch. "He deserves to know, if for no reason other than he needs to know where he stands. Whether he's your sub alone or it is going to progress to something more, something deeper."

"That's part of how the can got blown open this morning. My inability to sleep prompted his questions and while he didn't elaborate at the time, I could tell he had questions. It's going to come up, it's a matter of when and I just need to figure out how to tell him."

"Well, then maybe the pictures out there," he points down the hall with the knife, "Is the perfect opening point. Let it come out naturally. Let him ask you the questions. Your number one rule is communication so I know you won't be able to resist telling him about it."

I nod. "Can I help you with something?" I ask him, changing the subject and he frowns but lets it go before gesturing for me to come around the island and help him out.

Aryn

The tour of the house takes far longer than I'd expected but Will did a good job keeping us moving.

There are more pictures throughout the house. One in particular caught my attention in one of the sitting rooms. It was a huge portrait of someone who is obviously Teddy, one other male and the woman from the photos in the hallway who looks like she's maybe thirteen or fourteen and then what I'm guessing are Teddy's parents.

When we get to the hallway near the kitchen I stop at the far end and start looking at the pictures. One that catches my eye is of Teddy, the woman I keep seeing and then Caden standing in front of the Eiffel Tower in Paris. Caden looks younger, maybe ten to twelve years or so, Teddy too for that matter. "Who is she?" I ask Will.

"That's Daddy's sister."

"What's her name?" I don't know what possessed me to ask that question, but I guess I'm curious.

"Michelle."

"She's very pretty," I say absently.

"She is." I get the impression from Will's hesitation that I'm making him uncomfortable. I look over the pictures a little more until I find one of Michelle and Caden kissing and my heart aches.

"Where is she?" I ask Will.

"Will?" Teddy barks from the kitchen and Will bolts down the hall before he can answer my question. Damn it.

Not wanting to get Will or myself in trouble, I abandon the photos again in favor of the kitchen. But not before my eyes land on one final picture and my heart squeezes tight and falls into my stomach.

I do my best to let the picture out of my mind before entering the

kitchen with a smile on my face. "You have a gorgeous house, sir," I tell Teddy.

"Thank you, boy." I nod and smile at Caden who is still wearing that worried expression on his face but he still smiles at me from behind the island as he's helping Teddy with lunch.

"Can I help, sirs?" I ask.

"You can cook?" Teddy chortles.

"Uh, no. No, I can't." The three of them chuckle. "I guess living on the road as much as I tend to do, eating out is more second nature than actually cooking for myself."

"Come here," Caden says, and there is a command in his tone but it's still playful. The bantering about my lack of cooking skills has helped Caden's stress lower. Helping to make him laugh makes me feel less guilty about stopping to look at the pictures and my inadvertent probing of Will.

Though it desperately needs to be discussed and soon, I let it go in favor of having a good time with Caden, Teddy and Will. I stand next to Caden and start helping him chop vegetables for the salad he's making after he hands me a knife.

It's strange the way we seem to find a rhythm in the kitchen, almost natural, and I like it. Teddy and Will are working on the other stuff opposite us and there is a lot of banter back and forth between Will and Teddy and it's sweet to see. The way they pick on each other is comical and you can visibly see Teddy swell with pride over Will and I realize that I want that. Between Dex and Raine and now Teddy and Will, I can see that things like true love really exist in real life and it makes me want that more than anything.

I look at Caden who joins in their play from time to time, and for the first time since deciding to submit to him, I can see so much more between us and it makes me almost desperate for it.

CHAPTER THIRTEEN

*L*unch morphed into an all afternoon affair with Teddy and Will. We spent lunch bullshitting about life, the club, and me getting to know Will and Teddy a little bit more.

Will is a bit a wild child but the joy he brings to Teddy is palpable with each loving, adoring glance he gives him; even when I think he's being a bit of tool. Will is spunky and spontaneous and he has quite the sense of humor. He feeds Caden and Teddy in ways that I'm not sure I would ever see otherwise. It's very obvious to me that the three of them are the best of friends.

I found out that Teddy and Will have been together for about five years. Knowing that information and from the pictures I saw in the hallway, I am not sure Will ever knew Michelle, though I'm not certain. And given the way Teddy and Caden are together and the way he talked to me at the club, Teddy is loyal to Caden and I admire that.

Caden is also very animated, talking, joking and telling stories. You would think, given the history the three of them have, that I would have felt left out, but it was actually quite the opposite.

By the time Caden and I leave around six, I feel like I'm a member of their little group and that seems to animate Caden a little more. He takes my hand as we walk toward the car.

All I can really think about is talking to him about Michelle, but his mood seems lighter than it was after we first arrived and I'm not sure that's a boat I want to rock right now.

"Derek invited us to dinner tomorrow night," Caden says as he pulls out of Teddy's driveway.

"What did you tell him?"

"Well, I didn't want to commit to dinner with them, Dex and Raine included, if you weren't going to be here or if you had other plans."

"I have no other plans and I know you don't want to know this, but I'm here as long as you want me to be, or until the middle of March, whichever comes first."

His eyes dart to me quickly and then back onto the road. "What's in the middle of March?"

"A job," I state simply.

"What about Dex and Raine, before then?"

"Honestly, I haven't asked," I tell him.

"Maybe you should, just so I know how long I can keep you tied up." He gives me a wicked smirk and I know the wheels are turning in his head over the possibilities our time together can bring.

"I'll make a deal with you," I offer.

"I don't make deals."

"Okay, then how about this, I've made arrangements to handle Dex and Raine's return to Los Angeles and whatever else they need throughout the rest of the week. After that, let's just see how things go?"

"Are you putting a limit on our time together?" he asks as he pulls up to a stoplight. I look around, realizing that I have no idea where we are but we're in a very affluent neighborhood, similar to Teddy's but the homes are even bigger and I realize this could very well be the Hollywood of Nashville.

"No, Caden, I'm not. But eventually I will need to return to Los Angeles and my job, plus my apartment and things like that."

He frowns but nods before the light changes and he starts to go forward. I watch the houses as we pass them by, each one getting a little bigger or a little more hidden. The darkness outside the truck has the interior lights reflecting off the window and I can see Caden looking at me from time to time but he doesn't say anything.

After a few more houses he turns left and pulls up to a gate. He drops his window and types something into the key pad and the

gates swing open. My heart starts to sink as the visual of Caden's wealth comes into view. I feel very small the closer we get to his house.

Though still only a fraction of the size of Derek's two houses, Caden's house is right up there.

There are six or seven columns in the front, painted white with black shutters lining each window which is are all good size picture windows. I swallow hard. "You live here?"

He lets out a soundless laugh, "I do. This is my full-time residence."

"Where else do you have houses?"

I look at him and he hesitates to answer me. I'm not sure I understand why. "I have a condo in New York City, and a vacation home in Sydney."

"Huh," I breathe.

"What's that for?"

I chuckle a little, "I expected you to have one in Los Angeles, movie industry and all that."

"No, I have a beach house in Malibu," he says with humorous intentions and I groan. "What's wrong?"

"You realize that I make about a hundred and thirty grand a year, right?"

"Does it bother you that I have money?" He turns off the car.

"No, it's just I'm not used to it. Let alone all that comes with having piles of money."

"I'm not sure you could sit here with me if you were. Pretentious pricks piss me off."

My jaw falls slack. "I'm sorry, I didn't mean anything by that."

His eyebrows knit together. "I know you didn't and neither did I. Aryn, I spend money lavishly on my homes, maybe indulge a little in my cars, but I live a very low cost lifestyle because I'd prefer people not know that I have money, in fact I don't often share my job with anyone because I choose to be in the shadows. I like it there." He turns toward me. "Answer me something. How'd you assume that I have money? Besides the house."

"That night, the fetish ball, when Master Orik thanked his sponsors and he listed you with Derek, I guess I just assumed you did. Then there is your private room at the club. Derek has one, but it's not as big as yours. Not to mention the grand gesture of showing up in New York, then again in Sydney. Australia, especially, isn't exactly conducive to last minute trips being cost effective."

He laughs, "You're very observant. Does it bother you that I have money?"

"As long as you don't start throwing it at me, we'll be fine."

He laughs, "Good to know." He opens his door and moves to get out. "Come," he commands and I smile at the dominance returning. I open the door and climb out to meet him at the back of the SUV.

He grabs the infamous duffle bag and I pull my suitcase and laptop bag from the back and I follow him up to the house where he just turns the knob, opening to door. "You don't lock up your house?" I ask him.

He laughs, "Yes, of course, but I have this." He holds up a fob with a single button. He presses it and I hear the door click locked behind us and the telltale beeps of the alarm system engaging. "And it won't work unless I enter the code at the gate."

"Mills installed something like that in Talon's house. I never really understood all of it. Cameras on the other hand, I'm totally your man."

He chuckles. "I have plenty of those too. Come on," he says and he leads me to the left of the entry way and into a hallway that doesn't last but ten feet before it opens into a living room area. A very formal room at that. There is a fireplace and several expensive looking sofas and chairs spread throughout the room. It's nicely decorated but doesn't scream bachelor either. I follow Caden through the room to the opposite side from where we came in, to a door. He steps aside. "Open it," he tells me and I give him a sideways glance but do as he's told me.

I turn the knob and push the door open, but I stop myself from stepping inside because he's only told me to open the door. I assume he wants me to go inside, but this is my way of being a smart-ass. "Now what?" I chortle and he shakes his head laughing at me.

"Go inside," he says through laughter. I cross the threshold and the lights flicker on. I nearly drop my laptop bag on the highly polished wooden floor.

CHAPTER FOURTEEN
Aryn

Aryn's eyes roam around the room, taking in what I'm showing him, but there isn't a surprised look on his face like I'd expected. "You've seen a room like this before?" I ask him.

"Well, not exactly like this. I imagine Derek has one, though I've never seen it. Dex has one in his condo back in Los Angeles, but it is nothing like this either." His voice trails off as he takes in the room.

"I had this room done about three years ago," I tell him.

He steps into the room, leaving his suitcase and laptop behind as he walks along the walls. Lining the walls of my dungeon are various toys, whips, crops, floggers, paddles, you name it, they're all there. In between the racks of toys are a couple of different things, including a cross and the grid. Opposite all of that is a large four poster bed that has eight inch thick banisters and a solid metal frame at the top. The frame allows for cuffs, rope, or any other restraining device to be attached to it and it is strong enough to hold someone my size or larger. The bed is where Aryn stops. He takes in the detail of the posts and then his eyes follow them up until he sees the metal frame. A soft blush rolls over his cheeks and I can only imagine what's going through his mind as he takes it all in.

Next to the bed are a couple sets of drawers and some large mirrors, two attached to the walls and one free standing. Where we'd placed the wall mirrors (opposite the cross and grid) only made them accessible from those apparatuses, hence the free moving mirror.

Aryn's eyes wander to the mirrors. "I get the impression you like to watch?" His voice is soft, thoughtful.

I smile. "I do. I guess it's the voyeur in me." I hadn't made much of a secret about watching when I had him and Ash in my private room at the club.

"Any other fetishes that I should know about?" he asks, his voice more curious than concerned.

"Not that I've personally discovered, other than I like restraints, not a fan of masks-"

"Good, I'm pretty sure I can't do those."

"Have you ever tried?" I ask and he shakes his head. "You might be surprised," I tell him.

He shakes his head again. "Every time I've seen pictures or even a couple at the club, they put me on edge and make me uncomfortable and I'm not even the one wearing it."

I nod and give him a small smile. "Hard limit then?" I ask and he nods. "Noted. I don't like being cut off from lips or even eyes, but I can't promise not to blindfold you," I tell him and my mind starts wandering to him tied to the bed, his eyes covered.

"That I think I'm okay with," he breathes and I close my eyes as the vision of him restrained consumes me again, making my cock stir.

"Good," I finally breathe out. I pull in a deep breath, clearing my mind of the image he's given me, or at the very least, I do my best. "Come on, there's more to see," I tell him, needing to pull him from the room before I take him on the bed.

He gives me a knowing smile and while it should irritate me that he's seen my weakness, I find it oddly comforting that he seems to understand. My eyes roam down over his body, taking in his tight t-shirt, then the outline of a very impressive erection. I shiver in anticipation of what's to come between the two of us as I usher him from the room and close the doors behind us.

Aryn

Caden took me on a grand tour of his house and grand is by far an understatement. I lost count of how many bedrooms, rooms, and bathrooms along the way.

Now we're approaching the last door at the end of the hallway, it's closed, and unlike the rest of the doors in this hallway, he stands before it. I can sense a bit of hesitation before his hand goes to the knob to turn it open. "This is my room and where I would like you to stay while you're here."

"I don't mean to sound ungrateful, but are you sure? After last night, not being able to sleep..."

He gives me a serious look and states, "I know that I don't want you anywhere else but here."

I nod my understanding and he opens the door and pushes the light switch. Beyond the door surprises me. I'd expected a room and instead I am met with a wall and a step to the left. He leads us in, turning to the left and stepping up. I follow him up the eight or so stairs that lead to another wall at the top. It takes me only a moment to understand where his hesitation came from. It wasn't that he didn't want me in his bed, but the pictures that line the staircase. The elephant in the room is staring back at me with the brightest smile on her gorgeous face. A smile matched only by Caden who is next to her in the photo.

I shake my head, dispelling the inevitable conversation we're going to have about this and I imagine based on his demeanor at Teddy's earlier and now this that he doesn't want to talk about it.

Once Caden reaches the landing, he turns left again and disappears from my line of sight until I pull my eyes away from the walls and take the last few steps.

When I turn to my left, I am greeted with the largest bedroom I have ever seen in my entire life. It has to span at least a good three fourths of the house itself. On the far end is an opening in the wall met by a dark wood banister. Beyond it I can see into what appears to be a room below. One of the rooms we saw earlier. It was a great room and I remember thinking that the ceiling had to be as high as the house and I was right, though I didn't see the banister from down below.

My eyes wander back over the room. There are nearly a dozen windows lining both sides of the bedroom. I step into the room. To my left, about where the door downstairs is, there is another door, this one open and at this point I cannot see into it, but considering there doesn't appear to be an actual closet, I imagine that's it. Caden is standing off to my left, watching me as I take in the massive four poster bed. It has to be at least a California King or larger, covered in black silk with ice blue accents on the pillows. The floor is mostly a dark cherry hardwood, except for the area around the bed. Beyond the bed I see a sitting area with a few chairs and a massive over-stuffed couch.

"You could live in this room and never leave," I tell him.

"I often do," he tells me.

Opposite the sitting area is a massive work station that consumes that corner of the room. There appears to be no less than three computers and an empty spot in front of the chair with a stand in front of it for, my guess, a laptop. Along the wall opposite the bed are various pieces of furniture and all in all, it is simply designed but yet it screams Caden.

"You can put your stuff in here," he tells me as he ushers toward the door above the stairs. I set my laptop bag on a chair near the door and pull my suitcase behind me as he ushers me into the closet.

My eyes go wide when I take in the closet, pushing close to the size of my entire living room back home. There isn't a whole lot of empty space on the racks, but enough that I can hang some stuff up

and below that nearly empty rack is a luggage rack.

Caden takes my suitcase from me and places it on top of the rack. He doesn't say anything and I personally don't know what to say. When he's done he turns his back to me and walks toward the back of the closet. Then he turns left again and disappears through a door I hadn't seen when I'd come in. I follow him.

When I turn the corner, the closet opens into a massive bathroom. Double sink to my left, a toilet room straight ahead. To the right of that is a massive tub, as big as most hot tubs I've ever seen and between us and the tub is a glass enclosed shower that is at last three times the size of any standard shower. There are five shower heads inside, the one in the middle a massive rain shower head that looks too inviting right now.

"Say something," Caden says.

I look at him, he's concerned. "I honestly don't know what to say. I've never in my life seen a bedroom or a bathroom of this size before." I take a deep breath. "It's a bit overwhelming."

He gives me a small smile. "I understand. Even after all this time, I'm still not used to it." He gestures back toward the door. "Come on, you hungry?" he asks and I nod.

We leave the bedroom and make our way all the way down to the ground floor, three floors below his bedroom, and into the kitchen. "I have a staff, they don't work Sundays, but they will be here in the morning," he explains as he pulls some things from the fridge and places them on the massive island in the middle of the kitchen. "They're pretty invisible, but I didn't want you to be alarmed if you ran into someone. There are three of them, one man, who is usually in the kitchen, and two middle-aged women who clean up the house."

I nod.

He goes back to the fridge and grabs a couple things from the door and returns to the island. He pulls a bottle opener from a drawer and pops the top off before sliding a beer across the way to me. "Sit," he tells me and I take the beer and a seat on one of the stools in front of me. "You look like you have a lot on your mind, care to share?" he asks before taking a long pull from the beer in his hand. I can tell he's nervous but I have to ask him about her. I need to know, but I'm unsure of how to bring up the subject.

"How long have you lived here?" I ask, hoping for some insight without going at it head on.

"Fifteen years. It was my first major purchase after college. I got a smoking hot deal on it and as my career took off, so did the house."

That isn't very telling, but after gauging the pictures at Teddy's house and even the ones here, I imagine that whoever she is or was to him, she lived in this house at some point.

"How old are you?" I ask him.

He smirks, "Does it matter?"

I shake my head. "Not at all, just with the amount of time you seem to have put into stuff, it makes me curious."

"I'm thirty-eight," he tells me and my eyes widen.

"I'd have never guessed."

"You?" he asks casually.

"Thirty-four," I tell him before drinking more of my beer. It's imported and damn good, I take another sip.

"How long have you been a bodyguard?" His casual tone is a comfort and I watch as he sets about preparing dinner.

"I've worked for Bold ten years. I've been an official bodyguard for eight, about."

"What did you do before that?" he asks.

"I was in the Army. Enlisted at eighteen, served my two and reenlisted. I would have stayed in a lot longer but I got hurt and they wanted to throw me behind a desk."

He snorts, "That's not something I can ever see you doing."

I laugh too. "You're right. The desk job was optional and temporary, so I took it, sucked at it and hated every minute of it, but by the time things had been straightened out and I'd sat behind that desk, it was simply to ride out the remaining four months of my enlistment. The only perk to the desk job was I got to stay stateside. When my enlistment was up, I didn't re-up. Much to the disappointment of my C.O., but he understood that I wasn't meant for desk duty."

"What did you do in the Army?" he asks.

"Ranger."

He drops the spatula in the pan he was cooking hamburger in and looks at me in shock. "No shit?"

I smile. "That's how I got hurt."

"How so?" he asks has he picks up the spatula again and stirs the meat.

"On a drop in. They dropped us into the water because the terrain and winds were too rough to set down or for us to drop in. So we jumped in. I, unfortunately, had the lovely pleasure of meeting rocks under the water." I stand up and walk around the island, setting my beer down next to his and I pull up my right pant leg.

"Good Lord," Caden exclaims as he takes in the sight of the scar that runs up my leg from mid-calf to my knee. The line has faded considerably over the years and my dirty blonde hair keeps my leg hair light in color so it isn't visible unless pointed out. That was at least one thing the doctors got right when patching me up.

"Not only did it tear me up, but it broke both bones in my leg just below the knee. I had to have surgery, three times, and I was nearly immobile for about a year. After that it was physical therapy and by the time I was cleared to return to duty, so to speak, my time was nearly up and I could no longer jump."

"That's a bit of a requirement."

"It is. So I got injured in the line of duty without the lasting effects of combat. It was a win-win."

"Does it bother you now?" I drop my pant leg and grab my beer before returning to the stool.

"Occasionally, especially if I'm running without a brace on. But for the most part, it will ache in bad weather from time to time and after long days of being on my feet, ice is sometimes required." I shrug. "But other than that, no." I polish off my beer and set the bottle on the island while Caden finishes up whatever it is he's making. It smells delicious, whatever it is.

"That was probably the best spaghetti I've ever had," Aryn praises as he pushes his empty plate away.

"Thank you," I smile.

We've been chatting for a while now, just about little things. The things we like, music we enjoy and even some things we like to do in our free time. I was surprised to learn his previous habits usually involved random women and bars, but then again, the way he looks at me when I'm touching him speaks louder than he does. It tells me he's spent a good portion of his life avoiding attachment, commitment and longevity when it comes to any relationship. By the sounds of things, Dex and the guys he works with, Rusty and Mills, are probably his longest friendships.

"Tell me about your family?" I ask as I pick up my glass of wine.

He tenses on the other side of the table. He's obviously uncomfortable with the question I've asked him. "What do you want to know?" he deflects.

"Sisters? Brothers?"

"One each, they're half siblings." His answer is clipped and I realize this subject is going to be like pulling teeth.

"Younger? Older?" I push, willing to give him some patience with his answers, and a chance of settling into this discussion. I know it won't be easy for him when I see a brief look of exasperation cross his face. Though he stops short of rolling his eyes.

"They're both younger, by quite a bit. I haven't seen either one of them in over ten years," he offers without any prompting from me, but he doesn't offer any more. I can assume there is a reason why he hasn't seen them; a reason I can only guess at. "Though I talk to my sister about once a month," he adds and I give him a reassuring smile. Hoping to encourage more from him and he doesn't disappoint. "We only really communicate through email. It's been something we've done since I left. Except while I was enlisted when we could only communicate through written letter." He stops there; a far-off glaze fills his eyes as if he is remembering something. Whether it is about his service or about his sister, I'm unsure, but the distraction is definitely there.

"What about your parents?" I ask, hoping maybe changing the subject from his sister will wake him back up.

"What about them?"

"Are they still alive?" I ask.

"My mother is, my father I have no idea and I don't care." His tone is even more clipped and agitated than it was when I was asking about his siblings and I see that I'm pressing onto the real reason for his distraction or his anger.

"So, he wasn't around?" I counter and he shakes his head. "Does that piss you off?" I add.

He stands from the table and grabs his plate and glass. "It's hard to be pissed off at a man you've never met. He was gone before I was born."

"That makes it just as easy to be pissed off about, even now. You've never tried to look for him?"

He sets his dishes down in the sink and lowers his head. "No and he's never come looking for me either. If he didn't care enough then, he isn't going to care now. I know that people change their minds, change what's in their heart about things they've done in the past, but what I know about him tells me there is little to no chance of that ever happening. A fate I accepted a long time ago."

"That I can understand and I can see why you wouldn't want anything to do with him."

"There was a time, once, that I thought about tracking him down, but..." His voice trails off.

"But?" I prompt after a minute more of silence and he turns to face me.

He lets out a deep breath before he elaborates, "But I knew how it would go, if I managed to find him, and I knew it wouldn't be the warm welcoming I wanted."

"How do you know that?"

He shrugs. "I don't, but I realized it wasn't the right thing for me to do, and the next day I enlisted."

"So, you ran away from it?" I say to him as a question.

"I ran away from my father? Not really, you can't run away from something that isn't there. No, I ran away from homelessness."

My jaw falls open and I stare blankly at him, unsure of what it is I can ask him as a follow up to that. Unsure if he is willing to tell me anything, and praying like hell that he continues on his own.

"I need a drink."

I manage to pull my mouth shut. "Will you keep talking?" I ask him.

He gives me a coy smile. "Alcohol may make me easy, but it doesn't loosen my lips," he tells me and I walk toward where he's still leaning against the sink. I approach him, shifting the look in my eyes to more of a sultry one and he shivers and his mouth falls slack.

"I bet I can loosen up those lips," I tell him as I take the last two steps to press up against him.

He smirks. "Oh really?" he counters in challenge.

"Oh yeah," I murmur before pressing my lips to his. His lips open for me and I slide my tongue in along his, capturing the remnants of the last drink of wine he had and savoring the heady taste that is Aryn. The taste I've been unknowingly missing all day. I slide my hand up the back of his head into his hair and I tighten my grip. Pulling his head back, peeling his lips from mine and making it easier for me to kiss along his neck.

Between kisses, I ask him, "Why" kiss "were you" kiss "homeless?" kiss.

His voice is breathy when he answers, "Because I kicked the shit out of my mother's husband..."

That pulls me up short. There are only a few things that would incite that kind of reaction in Aryn and I know this because it's his nature. "Why?" I ask him, concern in my eyes when his eyes meet mine.

"Because he was raping my pre-teenage sister..."

I gasp and step back, releasing him. "No wonder you didn't want to talk about it," I mumble.

"It's alright, he never touched me and after I beat the shit out of him, he never touched her again."

"I'm sorry that it came to you doing that in order to get him to stop," I tell him before I wrap my arms around him, holding him to me. "Tell me the story?" I ask.

He nods. "But with a drink and somewhere more comfortable than the kitchen."

I smile at him. "You got both." I cock my head, indicating to him that I want to kiss him and he presses his lips to mine. This kiss is softer, and slightly less passionate, but no less arousing.

We both pull back after a few heartbeats and then I take his hand in mine, leading him into the room next to the kitchen. It's a wine cellar, filled with wine and just about any other alcohol you can think of. "Pick something."

"You have a preference?"

I smile, "Nope."

He casually looks around the room, checking out the different bottles. Everything from vodka to whiskey. Vintage and recent. He reaches into an unmarked wooden crate and pulls out a bottle of Pappy Van Winkles Family Reserve and inspects the bottle.

"Best whiskey around," I tell him. "Ever had it?"

He shakes his head. "Never heard of it, but is there any place better than Kentucky to make whiskey?"

I laugh, "No, there most certainly is not." He holds the bottle up, asking for my permission and despite the twenty-four hundred dollar price tag; he's completely worth it so I nod my head. He smiles and comes toward me, handing me the bottle.

"I'll let you do the honors," he says with a smile and I take the bottle from him before we leave the cellar.

I grab two lowball glasses from the sideboard in the living room. I'd thought about taking him to the sitting room, but I'm not sure I can be that close to my playroom with him right now. Especially if he clams up on me. I really want to hear what he has to say and in order to do that, I have to maintain control of myself, as hard as that might be.

I pull off the wax seal and unscrew the top, setting it down to breathe for a minute. I turn around to find Aryn wandering around the room. Once again, I see his eyes land on a picture of me and Shelly. Despite our free flowing conversation, I can sense there is an underlying elephant that has landed between us tonight.

I turn back around, realizing that I need this drink almost as much if not more than he does.

I look over my shoulder and he's still looking at the picture. I swallow hard. "Her name is Michelle," I say without looking at him. I don't have to see him to know he's turned around and is observing me. I pour two fingers into each glass and watch the amber liquid swirl and settle. The second glass settles and I add, "She's my wife."

CHAPTER SIXTEEN

My heart stops in my chest at Caden's confession. From all the pictures of her, I could gather that much, but to hear him actually admit it out loud is something completely different and I'm starting to wonder if I've made the right choice. Since I decided on this adventure with him I haven't second guessed myself until right now and I don't like it.

I can see him taking a few deep breaths before he finally turns around carrying two glasses in his hands and I'm more than ready for that drink now. He comes toward me, fear and sadness etching his eyes. They're full of moisture, though it hasn't spilled over. He hands me my glass. "I know you want to down that, but don't. It's ridiculously smooth, but it will knock you on your ass." His voice is full of the unspoken emotions portrayed in his eyes.

I nod my understanding and I take my glass from him. My fingers brush over his and there is a spark that ignites and my heart restarts itself.

I bring the glass to my nose, taking in the rich scent. "I've never had twenty-three year old whiskey before," I breathe.

"This is almost twenty-eight." He tries to smile but it comes across a bit weak.

I press the glass to my lips and my eyes never leave his as he watches me tilt the glass and the liquid slides over my tongue. Smooth is an understatement, but it has the unmistakable whiskey taste that I love so much. "Wow," I breathe when the liquid slides down my throat, warming me all the way down. Caden does the same, though he takes a bigger pull than I did, either because he knows what to expect or because he's opened up a can of worms he wishes he could close, but I'm not sure I can let him.

"Tell me, please?" I ask him.

He pulls in a very long, deep breath before stepping back from me and turning back into the room. I lean back against the table behind me. "What do you want to know?" he asks.

"I'm not sure what to ask in all honesty. I get from the look in your eyes that this story isn't a happy one. Given that this place screams bachelor, I'm guessing that you and her are no longer together and that scares me."

"Why would it scare you?" he counters. His probing about my family gave me the true reality of what he means by communication. He wanted enough information from me before he would let it go and while we're no longer talking about me, he's certainly not done.

"Because, either she's out there somewhere and you're still in love with her or-" I can't even bring myself to say it.

"Your idea of 'or' would be correct, Aryn."

My heart sinks into my stomach. This morning comes flooding back to me... "I haven't slept with anyone in ten years." That is immediately followed by the fact that in Teddy's house there are no pictures of Will, Teddy, Caden & Michelle.

"How?" I breathe.

Despite being a good distance away from me, the silence of the house makes even the softest whisper ring through the space.

"Car accident," is all he offers and I'm willing to take that answer, for now.

In a dual purpose of trying to convey to him that I want to keep this conversation going between us, I offer him a bread crumb. "When Alyce was nine or so, my mother's husband started sneaking into her room at night, while she was sleeping."

He turns to me, fear and overwhelming concern fill his too wide grey eyes.

"While it took me a long time to figure out what was actually happening in there, I knew it was happening and I started to do everything I could to stop it. I'd stay up late at night and wait for him to attempt to sneak into her room. Usually if he saw me or saw that I was still awake, I could scare him back into his own room. Though he wasn't very bright." I take another sip of the whiskey in my hand and this time it's much bigger. I swallow it down quickly. Feeling the burn of alcohol as it slides down my throat, taking comfort in the pain it is providing me gives me what I need to go on. "Then, as I got a little older, I started working more, graduated high school and wasn't around as much, so he took to getting to her during the day, after school." My hand tightens into a fist around the glass.

"Easy there, that's crystal," Caden says as he gestures to my hand. My knuckles are white from the strain I'm putting on them and before I can shatter it, I set the glass down on the table behind me and start to pace. "What happened after that?" he asks me and out of nowhere it all starts to spill.

"I'd gone to my mother, for the third time. Each time she failed to believe me, choosing her douche of a husband over her own children because the arrogant asshole would deny it and anytime anyone brought it up to Alyce; she wouldn't say anything at all. But the fear was always there and my mother failed to see it. Each time I'd told my mother about it, he'd settle down for a month or so before it would become too much for him and he'd be right back in the room."

"Why didn't you report him to child services?"

I snort a humorless laugh and look at him. "I did, four times. The final time they told me to stop making false reports."

"Those fucking morons." Caden's face slowly grows red with anger at each passing line of this story.

"They came out after the second accusation and between my mother, the douche and my brother Alyx, they denied anything was going on. Alyce was clearly traumatized when she was asked the questions about it, but they weren't convinced. So they left and left her to be further tortured by my mother's husband," I explain.

"How'd it finally stop?"

"I purposefully went home early from work, having figured out his pattern. When I got there he'd just gone into her room. He didn't know I was home." I return to the table and pick up my glass, slamming back the last little bit of whiskey in it before I turn around to face him. "I gave him enough time to drop his pants, and nothing more. When I heard him use his standard line about her getting naked, I pushed open the door and slammed him into the wall. I kicked the shit out of him. Caught him with his pants around his ankles and my mother still didn't believe me. Or at the very least, she still chose the deadbeat over her kids. I warned the son of a bitch that if he put his hands on her again I would kill him. Given that I'd nearly done so already, he believed me. That didn't stop my mother from kicking me out of the house."

"How old were you?"

"I was twenty when I was kicked out. I'd stayed behind with community college just so I could stay home and help protect her. Alyce was twelve at that point."

Caden shakes his head slowly back and forth, closing his eyes as he takes in my story. It never impacted me, at least not beyond what had happened with Alyce. "I'm not sure I'll ever forgive myself for not stepping in sooner."

"You did what you could, Aryn, don't blame yourself for that."

I scrub my hand through my hair. "I know that, but it doesn't stop me from feeling the blame, feeling as though I could have or should have done something sooner."

"But you did what you had to do. Who's to say if you'd done anything earlier that he would have stopped?" He takes a few steps in my direction. "He may have continued no matter how many times you beat his ass, or if your mother was so determined to protect him, she could have kicked you out sooner."

I nod as he steps closer to me. "I've heard it all before, and you're right. I don't know how things would have turned out if I'd acted sooner. But I know that Alyce is a mess now. It's completely ruined her."

"Whether it happened once or a hundred times, it would have had the same impact on her."

I nod my agreement and understanding.

"She was the love of my life," he breathes. "It's because of her that I've detached myself from everyone, never slept with anyone until last night. I miss her every day."

He's standing close enough for me to reach out and take his hand, so I do. I pull him toward me. He comes willingly and I wrap my arms around him. "I'd be more surprised if you didn't miss her," I breathe. My heart aches for him. Underneath that ache lies the fear that he won't be able to let go of her enough to let me inside.

"She's a beautiful woman," I tell him and he smiles a little at me.

"She was perfect."

"How does Teddy play into all this?" I ask and he doesn't answer, just cocks his head in confusion. "I saw the pictures in his house."

He nods with a sad smile. "Shelly's his sister."

"Oh." That clears up Will's statement back at their house.

He grins at my shock. "Teddy was how I met her, my senior year of high school, she was a freshman. I'd seen her, of course, but it wasn't until I went to Teddy's house a few months into the school year that I'd actually met her. They'd just moved to Nashville and Teddy and I just clicked together easily. The rest, as you can tell, is history."

I giggle a little. "I don't picture Teddy being very understanding of you dating his sister."

Caden laughs at that comment and he kisses me gently on the lips. "Oh, he wasn't, not in the slightest. But I think the more he got to know me, the more he saw that I wasn't able to just forget about her, and there wasn't much he could do. Eventually I proved to him I was a good guy with good intentions."

"She sounds like an amazing woman."

His smile turns sad and small. "She was."

Caden

Telling Aryn about Shelly is liberating and not something I expected. Though I haven't told him everything, I've told him enough that he doesn't have to carry around the questions about her that I can sense he has. But I also understand that it's opened up the chance for random questions going forward and I'm surprisingly okay with that.

What his sister went through isn't something I ever expected to hear from him, but I guess it just goes to show that you're never more than one degree away from an abuse victim.

"Want another drink?" I ask him, trying to change the subject, lighten the mood. This certainly wasn't what I had planned for tonight.

He smiles and leans in to kiss me again. "I'd love one," he tells me as he releases me and I'm surprised by the shiver of loss that slides up my spine but I grab his glass and return to the sideboard, this time filling it with three fingers worth. I look at my watch and find it's nearly ten o'clock.

When I return to him, he's watching me, as if he's checking to make sure I'm okay and I find comfort in that. "I need to go upstairs. I've been away from my email more than twenty-four hours and I need to..."

He smiles. "Say no more." He gestures toward the door of the living room and I lead him back to the top floor of the house.

"Please don't take this the wrong way, but are you sure you want me sleeping up there with you?"

I pause briefly before opening the bedroom door. "I was sure before I told you, and I'm even more sure now." I take a deep breath and admit, "I've never told anyone what I've told you tonight."

He can't hide his surprise. "Not even Ashley? Your other subs?"

I shake my head. "No, Aryn, I've kept them at arm's length, never getting closer. Ashley is the only one who ever stepped foot in my house until you and that wasn't all that long ago. I cannot imagine you sleeping anywhere else."

He smiles and nods. "Good, because I don't want to sleep anywhere else."

I smile at him and open the door. This time I follow him up and I can't help taking in the pictures that line the stairwell walls. All the pictures of Shelly and me. How could he not ask about her with all this staring back at him as he steps up the stairs? I do notice this time that he's not looking at them, at least not obviously. I gave him no choice but to ask the questions he did tonight. Between Teddy's house and here, he was bombarded by it and that actually makes me feel a bit guilty. I should have found a way to explain first.

"I should only be a few minutes," I tell him when we reach the bedroom.

"I'm going to go hop in the shower, if that's alright?" he asks.

"You should take a bath, much more fun." I wink at him and he lights up a little. I threw just little bit of a tone in there to show him that is what he should do. We will see if that's what he does.

"Yes, Master," he says with a smirk.

"Get," I tell him and he hops to it, disappearing into the closet before I make my way across the space and sit down at my desk to wake up one of my computers.

When I see more than a hundred new emails, I roll my eyes and open up my email program. While it loads, I hear one faucet, then another kick on from the bathroom and I smile.

Right where I want him.

CHAPTER SEVENTEEN

The giant tub, big enough for Caden's six-five frame to fit comfortably, fills with water from the three faucets that surround it. Watching the water swirl is hypnotic and it's making me think. The only thing that keeps swirling in my mind like the water in the tub is the fact that I feel like an ass for worrying about what Caden's wife means to him. The reservations I had going into this have been completely validated by the fact that he's unable to form emotional attachments. It's the reason he's turned to strictly sexual encounters and nothing further.

When he told me Shelly is no longer here, nothing else mattered except him. My heart broke for him, not just because he lost his wife, but because of the pain he's still in over her loss. But maybe a little for me too. I didn't decide to submit to Caden for a sexual thrill. I made my decision because there's more between us than just a Dom and his sub. At least that's the reason I keep trying to convince myself with. But am I enough?

I reach over to all three faucets and turn them off, then press a couple buttons on the panel in the wall, sending the tub whirling gently. The water is calm and inviting. The jets don't pierce the surface of the water but you can clearly see them moving under the water. I pull my shirt off then toe off my shoes before standing and stripping out of my jeans and boxers.

There is an empty shelf to the left of the tub so I fold my stuff and place it there.

My cock is hard still and it bounces uncomfortably as I climb into the tub. My first instinct is to grab hold of it and relieve myself of the hard-on, but I get the impression that just might piss Caden off and I can't have that. But I also don't want him to come in here when he's done and see that I'm hard as stone.

The water is warm, soothing even, as I settle down into it. I press

my back against one side and I close my eyes.

My mind wanders back to this morning when he woke me up. He promised to keep an open mind, to consider that there just might be more between us than just sex. The fact that I'm here, in his home and that he wants me to stay is another sign that I just might be freaking out over nothing. I've never done the relationship thing, never expected that I would do the whole dating thing, let alone with a man, but around Caden I can't think of anything else. I don't know why that is exactly; I just know that he does something inside me that I've never felt before.

Seeing him sends my heart racing, my stomach flutters like it's full of butterflies and being near him is almost like being home. It's unexplainable, but I knew the first time I met him this wasn't going to be something I could forget about, no matter how hard I tried.

This isn't just about being his submissive, it's about being his partner and I don't know how to prove that to him without pushing so hard that I push him away. But I am also not going to lose myself in the process. My desire to please Caden is the strongest feeling I've ever had in my entire life, but I'm also walking a fine line. If I let my desire to please him rule over everything else, I'm going to lose who I really am. But if I don't let the desire to please guide me, I don't know that I'll be the kind of sub he needs and wants. I feel like a whirlpool, just spinning in circles with no real answer at the end of it. At least for now.

"Penny for your thoughts?" Caden's voice makes me jump.

I open my eyes and look up at him. He's completely naked. My eyes roam over his well-defined chest and over his abs until they land on his rock hard erection standing at attention. I lick my lips. He smirks. "So it was one of those kind of thoughts," he teases and I'm relieved that my cock is hard, hiding my true thoughts from him. It's too soon to consider discussing this, we need time. I need time and most importantly, he needs time to know whether or not he can accept me for me and be with me.

I blush and divert my eyes, showing him my shyness, though I don't really feel shy, I just don't want him asking more questions right now.

"Sit up?" he asks, rather than demands and I smile, looking back at him as I grab the sides of the tub and sit up, giving him room. He steps in behind me, lowering himself into the water and sliding his legs along mine. Once he's situated, he grabs my shoulders and pulls me back against him.

He grabs a sponge off the side of the tub and dips it into the water in front of me before bringing it up and over my chest. "Now, what were you really thinking about?" he asks.

Dammit. I take a deep breath. "I want to be honest with you, but I don't want to..." I stop. Can I really do this? Can I really be this open with him?

"You don't want to, what?" he asks.

I sigh as he brings the sponge up and over my other shoulder. The rough texture of the sponge feels like sandpaper against my skin as tension rolls through my body. "I don't want to take this fast and yet I feel like I'm spinning out of control," I tell him.

He doesn't stop what he's doing and the tension starts to fade. "In what way?"

"Emotionally," I tell him honestly.

"Can you elaborate?" There is true curiosity in his voice which brings me a little bit of comfort.

I swallow. "I'm afraid that I'm getting emotionally invested in this, in us, too fast. That you're not ready to do the same," I blurt out in a rush.

His hand stills for a moment and the tension returns as panic rises. I move to sit up, to put some distance between us, but his arms wrap around me, holding me to him. "Don't." he breathes. "I need you to stay right here," he whispers.

"Okay," I say softly.

I feel his head press against the back of mine gently, his breathing is a little ragged behind me and I shift my head, putting it against his shoulder. My heart is racing in my chest, my breathing matches his and we're not even doing anything. Anticipation is killing me and patience isn't my strong suit right now.

"It's too soon," I breathe. "I'm sorry, I just...I'm just trying to compartmentalize the crazy emotions swirling around me." I start to ramble, "I understand about Shelly, about your past relationships. I get it. I guess I'm worried that this isn't any different for you than Ash or any of your other..."

"Stop talking," he says softly, not an order or malicious in any way.

His hand comes up to my chin and he turns my head toward him.

"I'm sorry, I..."

"Shhh," he hushes and presses his lips against mine at an awkward angle. I try and shift and he lets me so I roll over, pressing my lips harder to his. He nips at my bottom lip, coaxing me to open for him and I do. His tongue slides in along mine and I moan into his mouth. My cock is hard as steel, pushing the point of painful with a desperate need for release. He releases me from our kiss. "I need you," he breathes.

I cock my head. "You have me. I'm here."

"Good," he breathes before claiming my lips one more time. He releases my chin and I feel his hand slide down between us, then his fingers wrap around my cock and I moan.

I stop the kiss. "I'm on the edge," I warn him, and it's true.

"No rules," he breathes. "No roles, just you and me."

He presses his lips against me again as he grabs my cock more firmly before stroking upwards. I slide my hand up his thigh until I find his cock and I wrap my fingers around it, tugging gently. He trembles beneath me and he lets out a huge rush of air before pulling from our kiss and hissing through his teeth.

I want to do so much more to him, but the water is in the way. I sit up a little; his hand never stops stroking along my cock. I find the drain button and press it.

He looks at me quizzically and I smirk. "It's in my way," I explain.

The water drains from the tub quickly, the cool air around us sends shivers through both our bodies, but I'm determined to warm us both up as quick as possible.

The moment the water has drained enough to give me access I pull myself free of his hand and slide down his body. With his cock in my hand I look up at him as I dart my tongue out and flick it across the bottom of the head and he groans.

I smile before opening my mouth and sucking his entire head into my mouth. He bucks beneath me. I stroke up and push down with my hand as I suck on the head of his cock.

"Oh god," he groans. "So good."

The compliment sends a new wave of pleasure through me. My cock drips pre-cum and I use my free hand to stroke it, coating it in my fluids. Caden's eyes follow my movements and he's riveted to the sight of me stroking my cock in time to the sucking and stroking I'm giving him.

"Fucking gorgeous," he breathes and again I feel pleasure rising, my cock hardening, my balls tingling. My orgasm is close, but I want to make him come first so I release my dick from my hand and put more effort into what I'm doing to him.

I start sucking deeper, letting his cock reach the back of my throat before pulling up. He slides his hand into my hair to help guide me and the touch sends a shiver of desire through me. "Don't stop," he breathes.

I don't. I can't. I need this, he needs this. No rules, no roles, just Aryn and Caden. Caden and Aryn. Just us.

I slide my hand into Aryn's hair, holding him, touching him.

Tonight has been something I never expected.

I never expected to be able to tell him about Shelly, and though I haven't told him everything, it's enough that he now understands my reluctance and yet, here he is.

"That's it, baby," I breathe.

His mouth sucks a little harder on my cock, his hand strokes up a little harder, and fuck. I'm right there. I want to give in, give him what he so obviously wants, but I feel guilty - a whole new emotion for me.

He's shown me his heart and I'm allowing him to take from me when I should be doing this to him.

My balls tingle, my pleasure pools, ready to explode any moment and I can't fight it anymore.

"I'm gonna come," I grunt through gritted teeth and Aryn sucks harder, strokes faster. "Aryn," I cry out as my orgasm overtakes me and I empty down his throat. He sucks down every last drop, stroking and sucking me until I settle back against the side of the tub.

My eyelids are heavy. The lack of sleep is catching up to me, not to mention the alcohol we consumed, but I manage to open them and I see Aryn smiling at me. I move my hand to the side of his face. "You shatter me," I confess softly. "You break every rule I've ever laid down for myself."

"I don't mean to," he says hesitantly.

I smile at him. "It's not a bad thing," I reassure him. "I built walls, walls that I thought I was using to keep everything close to my heart. To keep all the things I thought I needed in life close and tonight those walls started to crack." I move my hand from his cheek; we both shiver from the cold. "You're the first person I've told about Michelle and I didn't realize, until I told you, that I was harboring those feelings so close to me. When I started to let them out, there was a huge weight that lifted from my shoulders." I keep my voice purposefully soft. He shivers again. "Let's dry off," I suggest. "There are a couple more things I need to tell you."

He gives me a reassuring smile with a nod as he stands up. Once he's steady, he reaches down for me. Oddly enough, I should be taking care of him, not talking about this. His erection is inches from my face and I can't help myself.

I grab hold of it. "You don't have…"

"Shhh," I tell him. "I want to, and then we can talk."

He nods and I stroke up on his shaft. The pleasure of my touch consumes him and his eyes roll upward. I smile to myself as press my lips to the tip of his cock before I suck it into my mouth. "Oh, god," he groans.

He's hard as stone. He's had this erection for some time and I get the sense that this isn't going to take long. That gives me a thrill of satisfaction as I start sucking and stroking his cock the way he did mine. After a few strokes, he slides a hand into my hair and I savor the contact. My own cock grows hard again. There's a shift between us tonight and tonight I need to be with just him. No rules, no roles, just us, and I will do whatever it takes to make that happen.

I suck a little harder and his cock twitches in my mouth. "So close," he breathes.

Good.

I continue for a few more strokes before I feel his hand tighten in my hair and his breathing alters, he grunts then says, "I'm coming." I stroke him harder, faster and he explodes down my throat. He tastes delicious and it's a taste I pray I never get enough of.

We climb out of the tub and dry off after we both catch our breath. I pull a pair of flannel pajama bottoms from my drawer as Aryn goes

to his suitcase in the closet. He too pulls a pair of pants from the bag and puts them on. Both of us have lost our erections but if he's feeling anything like I am right now, one idea or a simple touch will set us both off.

"You thirsty?" I ask him.

"I am." He smiles at me.

"What would you like?"

"Water would be great," he tells me and I go into the bedroom, moving around the bed to the sitting area where there is a small refrigerator and I pull out a couple bottles of water. When I turn back toward the closet, he's standing on the other side of the sitting area.

"Here." I hand him the bottle of water and he takes it from me.

"Thanks." He sets it down on the coffee table. "Come here," he says. I give him a raise of an eyebrow. "No roles, remember?"

I smile. "No roles," I remind myself and walk over to him. He takes my water bottle from my hand and puts it on the table with his before wrapping his arms around me.

Stepping into Aryn's arms is an unexpected comfort. A feeling of safeness and security envelopes me. I sigh as I wrap my arms around him. And he's right. There is much more between us than just a D/s relationship. He's never been just a sub to me and now, in this moment, I'm not sure I want him as my sub. I think I need him as something more.

I try not to blow off that idea, but I also know I'm feeling vulnerable and splayed wide open tonight and I can't let that rule me or us or where we're going with all this.

He pulls back and looks at me with a small, warm, reassuring smile and it hits me. Shelly was right. My eyes start to fill up and I pull back from him, grabbing my bottle and putting some distance between us. "She was right," I say out loud.

"About what?" he asks.

I turn the cap on my bottle and pull a big drink from it, swallowing it back as a tear slides down my cheek. I wipe it away, glad I'm facing away from him. "Happiness," I breathe.

"How so?" One of the chairs protests as he sits in it.

"This morning, I woke up because I had a dream. It's the same one I've been having for ten years. Shelly and I were in the same car." My side starts to hurt in sympathy, like it always does when I talk about this. "We were driving home from a doctor's appointment." Another tear slides down my cheek. "And every time I have the dream, the ending is always the same. It doesn't matter what I do in the dream to try and change the outcome, it's always the same. We get hit and she dies." The tears are streaming now. "But this morning was different."

I turn around to face Aryn, red-rimmed eyes and all. I see the pain in his eyes as he takes in my saddened state. He shuffles to stand up. I put my hand up to stop him. "I'm alright, I just..." I take a breath, "I haven't cried about this in a long time, so bear with me, please?"

"Always," he tells me as he settles back down.

"We were t-boned. Hit on the passenger side by a truck going more than double the speed limit, drunk and high on coke. Shelly was ejected from the car. She was killed instantly."

"Caden, I...I'm so..."

"Don't," I put him off. "It wasn't your fault, it wasn't mine, or hers. It took me a lot of time, money and therapy to be able to say that about what happened." Tears flow down my cheeks as I continue, "We'd just found out we were expecting a little girl. Shelly was four and half months pregnant."

"God, Caden," he breathes before tears well in his eyes.

"So," I say, no longer trying to hide the emotions, "Not only did I lose the love of my life, I lost my little girl. Teddy lost his sister and his niece. It was a mess, we were a mess." I give a humorless laugh. "We're still a mess, but we manage," I tell him. I take a seat opposite him. "It took some time, but eventually Teddy, already a member of the lifestyle, introduced me to it. He explained as much to me as he could, so I took on a submissive role, and in doing so, I discovered that I could let myself go, that I could forget it all if only for a little while. At first, when I would come back to reality, I was an emotional mess, destructive even. Eventually I found an outlet to relieve that emotional madness inside me. It usually involved boxing. Whether it was hitting a bag or fighting with someone. It didn't matter, but fighting someone gave me a high similar to being a submissive. It gave me a thrill to fight someone, to pour all my emotion into my fighting and I could walk away feeling relieved." I take another big gulp of water. "Eventually, I started topping from the bottom, a lot. I knew going into it that being a submissive was not for me, but I didn't know how else to release myself of the burden I felt. My Domme at the time realized she was no longer helping me as a submissive and she started training me as a Top. From the first time I cracked a whip, until this very day, I've never stepped foot in a boxing ring again.

"Am I a little sadistic? Maybe. I do enjoy the pain I cause a submissive, but not so much so that I wish them harm or to be scared or marred by my actions. Eventually I realized it was the sense of control giving me the high that I once found as a submissive, but it also gave me an outlet to channel my anger to more positive energy. Until you walked into that club, I never imagined finding more than a submissive. I never thought I could allow myself the emotional connection." I pause, taking a deep breath. "But with you, you destroy all sense of what I think I should do. You shatter my rules because from the moment I saw you, I knew you could never be just a submissive to me. Do I want you to submit to me? Yes, I do. But I also want the challenges I know you're going to bring me. I also know that I need to accept the fact that while I'll never forget about her and I will always love her, there will always be a part of her inside me but it doesn't have to stop me from finding happiness with someone else."

I stop talking, giving him a chance to digest my words. It doesn't take him long before he responds. "I can't replace her," he states simply.

"I don't expect you to."

He shakes his head slightly. "Good, because I can't replace her. I can't give you the things you had with her simply because I'm not a woman..."

"That's not..."

"Let me finish, please?" he pleads and I nod. He gives me a small smile and continues, "But that doesn't mean I want to stop where this is going. I know this is going to be a crazy train ride with you and I accepted that before I walked into the club last night. But it's a train ride I need to take, a ride I think we both need to take." He pauses and takes a breath. "I'm not asking for forever, Caden. I'm just asking for today, tonight, tomorrow, maybe next week. I want the chance to learn from you, the chance to be your submissive, the chance to be your lover. I just know that I have to have more than that with you. I want nights like tonight where we talk."

"Where we have no roles?" I ask.

He nods. "Exactly. I'm not sure I'm built like Will. I'm not sure I can submit to you every hour of every day, but if it's what you need, I'll do it. Just know it will be hard for me. I need to have a little control over my own life and I think that's what scares me the most about doing this," he tells me sadly.

I get off the chair I'm sitting in and walk over to him. I'm standing before him in a gesture of understanding. I lower myself to my knees between his legs. "I can't promise forever, but I can promise you today, tonight, tomorrow, next week and longer. I never expected you to submit to me all the time, just when I know it's best for you. Or when you give me the signs that you need me to take control. I would never ask you for more than you can handle, Aryn, not now and not anytime in the future." I take a deep breath and put my hands on his thighs. "The fact that you're still here, knowing what

106

you know, tells me I made the right choice in coming after you. In flying to Australia, in being at the club last night. I feel complete when I'm around you and the idea of you leaving hurts more than I could have thought possible."

He cocks his head at me. "Is that why you didn't want to know when I had to leave?"

I nod. "I didn't want time limits. But unfortunately I am going to have to set one."

"What do you mean?" He looks confused as he raises an eyebrow.

"I have to be in Los Angeles on Wednesday. But, I'm hoping that you'll come with me," I tell him.

He smiles, "Absolutely."

I smile back at him and rise up on me knees. "Good," I say as I slide my hands up his stomach, over his chest to his shoulders then finally to his neck before pulling him down to kiss me. His hands come up to my cheeks, cupping them and holding me to him. Our breathing spikes and he pulls back shaking his head. "What?" I ask.

"I don't like you on your knees," he smirks before he slides down onto the floor, putting us both on an even playing field.

I smile at him before pulling his lips back to mine.

After a few heartbeats, I stand, pulling Aryn up with me. "Come on," I whisper.

He stands up and follows willingly as I lead him toward the bed. I need to figure out how best to show him this is real and I'm going to do that the only way I know how. Right now, that means taking him to bed and showing him that dominating him is not the only thing I want from him. I want so much more than that and I think by doing this I am not only trying to prove it to him, but also to myself.

Shelly was, is and always will be the love of my life, but my dream this morning has shown me that I can still love her unconditionally forever and still find happiness with someone else.

I've been with countless woman and a couple of men, but none of them have made me feel this way about them, no one but Aryn.

Ashley came close, but for some reason I always felt like if I picked Ash, I would be settling. With Aryn I feel true happiness.

6 MONTHS LATER

It's been six months since the first night I spent at Caden's.
It's been a wild and crazy six months.

After that night, we spent the next day at Derek and Dacotah's
with Dex and Raine. We had a wonderful time and it was clear that
friendships were forming and bonding the six of us together, not
just because of the lifestyle, but because we all blended together
well. It was a little odd at first, being on the inside instead of the
outside with Derek's main security man, Sean. He and I caught up
for a few minutes and it was great to see him again. It wouldn't be
the last time I'd see him as business has frequently brought Derek
to Los Angeles over the last few months. Cotah always comes along
with him so that she and Raine can spend time together. I didn't
quite understand it, but there was a special bond between the two
of them.

It also took three trips of me out with the girls, at Derek's request,
before I really realized what he was doing. He was putting the three
subs together, giving us a chance to hang out and bond a little. It
was awkward after I figured it out and Caden and I had spent a
couple hours discussing how important it was to bond with them.

I'd rolled my eyes because the girls' idea of bonding usually
involved shopping. When I told Caden that, he chuckled a little
bit at that but then he reminded me that even though they
were shopping, the three of us were talking, despite my role as
bodyguard. The girls accepted me into their little 'subbie circle' with
ease. I was just another sub, a friend and a confidant they both
grew to trust and enjoy having around. And I enjoyed them as well.

Caden and I returned to Los Angeles the day after the one we spent
at Derek's house because Cay had to get back to work. Yes, I've

given him a nickname and he loves it. It was just something that slipped out about three months ago and it's stuck around since then.

Caden returning to work was the start of our wild whirlwind.

He was leaving, heading to Beijing and then on to Berlin for the filming of his latest project. He practically begged for me to go with him, but I couldn't. Dex and 69 Bottles needed me and the only way I could go with him was if I quit my job. Though Cay and I talked about it extensively, he understood my need to work, my need to have things outside of our bedroom to keep me occupied. He followed up his asking me to go with him and my subsequent denial with asking me to move in with him.

Needless to say, I panicked at the prospect of moving out of my apartment, despite spending every possible minute with Caden at his house, I still had a place to call my own. We'd argued back and forth about it, but in the end I explained to him that being in his house, living there, without him there, made me uncomfortable.

The conversation continued into his fears for my safety and my being alone when he couldn't be with me and he'd be a world away. When I discussed it with Dex, he turned to Caden and offered up the spare room in his and Raine's apartment as an alternative. Dex offered Caden his protection of his sub and Caden accepted his offer.

Though I was reluctant at first, I did eventually move into Dex and Raine's house. Caden left me with strict rules and one of them included that Dex, though not my Master, is still a Dom and I was to respect him for that. I was also to accept any further training from Dex when it was offered.

I was worried that Dex would take it to a level of uncomfortable, but he never did. I was free to come and go as I pleased. I was also free to do as I wished, but if I didn't follow the rules, then Caden would hear about it and he did hear about it more than a few times.

I never realized I could be lonely. But I was, very much so, with Caden gone for work. Dex sensed it and told Caden. I knew he knew because Caden flew home immediately and he stayed with me for about thirty-six hours before he had to return to Beijing. Again he begged me to come with him. My resolution about staying and working faltered. I nearly quit because the idea of being lonely and being without Caden, again, was nearly unbearable.

That night, before he left, he took me to Dex's private playroom and he took our relationship to a whole new level. It was also the first time I soared into subspace. When it was all said and done with, I was reminded of my place in Caden's life and I never felt more loved and adored when it was all over. That brought me comfort for the next couple of weeks before he moved onto Berlin. Once he was there, our communications became more frequent because the time between us wasn't so dramatic. It was easier to talk to him regularly and it helped curb my loneliness.

June rolled around and Caden was trying to wrap up his filming, but it was taking longer than he'd planned. Dex, Raine and 69 Bottles had plans to go to Phoenix for Cami's birthday. Caden surprised me when he showed up in my hotel room the night before.

We spent the first night wrapped in each other's arms reconnecting with one another. It came second only to the first night we spent at his house in Nashville six months ago. The next night, after the party ended and we were squared away in our room, I was promptly tied to the bed and made to soar again.

The day after that, Dex and the band returned to Los Angeles and Cay and I stayed locked away in our room until Monday when he flew back to Berlin and I returned home to Los Angeles.

It was getting harder for him to go and leave me behind. This time he didn't ask me to come along and I was grateful that he hadn't. I don't know if I'd have had the strength to deny him again. Only that time I really didn't have a choice. Work was calling. 69 Bottles

was getting ready to go on an appearance tour. They had a schedule of appearances ranging from radio stations, to TV shows, to festival concert shows and I was looking forward to the trip. The chance to get away from Los Angeles and even more so, the chance to find myself.

After Caden left Phoenix, I felt lost, confused and my heart ached. It took me a long time to figure out the reasons behind it all because it had nothing to do with Cay. Well, actually, it did, in a way.

While we were in Phoenix, we learned of Cami, Ireland – Cami's half-sister-, and Cotah's pregnancies and that has made it difficult to stop thinking about my future, our future. I know we've only been together for a few months, but there was more happening between us than I could have ever imagined.

But what's next?

Where do we go from here?

I'm learning more and more about the lifestyle with each passing day, not only from Caden, but from Dex and Raine. However, Caden and I are not lifestyle all the time. Which is a relief and it makes me happy. It's like he knows when I need his dominance and I blossom under it. At least that's what he tells me.

But the talk about our future together is coming and it's going to have to happen. I think I've decided what it is that I want in my life, but I have no idea how Cay feels about it. I hate to get so deep with him, but I need to know where we stand and where we're going from here.

That's how I've ended up driving through Nashville on my way to Caden's house. I flew in just a little over an hour ago because Caden is coming home and he requested I come here. Actually, he sent an airline ticket to my mailbox and demanded I come here instead of him coming to Los Angeles.

He called me on a video call about ten seconds after I received the

email and I asked him why here and he promptly told me that he can fly to Nashville faster than California and he needs to see me, badly.

I told him that he was lucky I could take the time off.

For which he promptly scowled at me, giving me his Dom stare. Despite the glass screens between us, it was no less powerful and the look had me desperate to slide to my knees and apologize to him. He knew it too when his gaze softened and he told me that he'd see me the day after at his house in Nashville.

So here I am, on my way to his house in Nashville.

My heart is racing in my chest despite the fact that I know he's not home yet. He won't be home until tomorrow, but wanted me here so I could pick him up at the airport tomorrow when he landed. I plan to be at the exit when he gets through customs.

I turn down his street and my breathing spikes, my heartbeat kicks up a notch. I haven't been here since we left for Los Angeles six months ago. Sadness slices through me when I realize that he's not going to be here. The knowledge that I'm going to spend the next twelve hours in his home without him has my heart seizing in my chest.

Pulling up to the gate and the keypad, I roll down my window and press in his code. It's Michelle's birthday. The gates swing wide and I drive my rented SUV up the driveway. The external lights of the house come on and I know that the security system is shutting down for me to go inside. I park near the garage and climb out of the car before grabbing my bag from the back and closing the gate.

As I approach the house, something seems a little off. I can't quite comprehend it. But it has me reaching for my gun under my arm and I click off the safety as I approach the house.

Once at the door, I fling my bag over my shoulder so I can grab the knob and I do exactly that, turning the knob and the door opens. The code at the gate did what it's supposed to do and unlocked the

front door. Once I open the door, my breath seizes in my chest.

Beyond the door is complete darkness except for a pathway of candles that lead from the doorway into the formal sitting room and beyond.

I holster my gun, set my bag down, close the door and set the alarm before following the path into the living room. When I round the corner, the path leads directly to the open door of Caden's playroom.

I can't stop my feet. My heart rate speeds up again. Each step I take draws me closer to the open door. I don't know what to expect beyond it, but regardless, there's only one explanation for it. Caden is home and I desperately want to see him, hold him, touch him.

I step into the playroom and it's empty, but there are more candles that lead me to a dresser on my left. I walk to it and look down.

Sitting atop the dress is a note.

> Strip, my sweet slut.
> Kneel by the door and wait for me.

My eyes move from the note to the top of the dresser and my heart freezes in my chest when my eyes land on a coiled up whip.

I shudder.

Caden has been working me toward expanding my pain threshold during the times that we've been able to play, but I don't know if I'm ready for this level of pain.

Realizing that Caden has given me a command to strip and wait for him and that my standing here is delaying seeing him, I pull my jacket from my shoulders, folding it nicely and laying it on top of the dresser. I move to my shoulder harness for my gun and remove it from my shoulders and set it on the dresser before I pull my gun from the holster and pull the slide back, releasing the bullet from

the chamber and then the clip before setting them back on the dresser in the holster.

I strip off my t-shirt and then unbutton my jeans before pulling off my boots and kicking off my jeans and boxer briefs.

I turn around, my eyes roaming over the playroom to find something out of place, but I didn't get a chance to play in here so I can't honestly tell if anything is missing or moved. But what I do notice is that the longer my eyes roam around the room, the harder my cock grows.

I complete my tasks by stepping over the candle line and heading for the door. Once there, I lower myself to my knees. Touching my butt to the heels of my feet, I spread my legs before I place my hands flat against my thighs.

My cock throbs, my heart races and my mind roars a million miles a minute.

He's here, he's home and he's not holding back.

Fear for our discussion bubbles briefly but I tramp it back down. Tonight isn't going to be the night, it never was. He wasn't supposed to be here, but my heart picks up in triple time when I realize that he is here. I get to see him, touch him.

I lower my chin to my chest and try my best to calm my breathing. To bring myself to the here and now and to find my happy place.

I'm so lost in my thoughts about what's going to happen that it isn't until I feel his hand slide into my hair that I know he's here.

"Hello, my sweet slut." My heart races again and my breathing hitches in my throat as my Master has returned.

"I missed you, Master."

His hand tightens in my hair and I shiver. His touch is obliterating all worry that I thought I had about seeing him.

"I've missed you, pet," he says confidently as he lowers himself next to me. Once he's settled, his hand in my hair tugs, pulling my face toward his. I keep my eyes cast downward as I've not been granted permission to look at him. "You please me, pet. Now, raise your eyes and look at me," he commands and my eyes open slowly until they meet his. His are warm, loving, adoring, and intoxicatingly sexy as a shiver of anticipation slides through me. "Tell me, my sweet slut, are you ready to soar for me?"

"Yes, Master," I breathe.

"Are you ready to burn for me?"

"Yes, Master," I answer with a little more confidence.

"Are you ready to suffer for me?"

My cock twitches. "Yes, Master."

His other hand grabs hold of my cock, stroking it from base to tip, and he pulls my face closer to his. "Good," he breathes before slanting his lips over mine and stealing a soul-quenching kiss from my lips. I whimper into his mouth and he swallows my moans with each stroke of my cock and each flick of his tongue against mine.

I cry out in frustration as my orgasm rages just beneath the surface.

Caden immediately recognizes the signs and pulls back from our kiss and he releases my cock. "Well done, pet." His voice is soft, soothing and just what I needed to hear to let my heartbeat return to normal. I wasn't granted permission to come for him and I've learned that coming in his hand is never something Caden wants.

"Thank you, Master."

He stands and reaches into his pocket, pulling something from it. I can't see what because I've lowered my eyes to the ground as I've been trained. As much as I hate not being able to look at him, I know that my doing as I'm told, without actually being told, pleases him.

I didn't expect him to show up here tonight, and I know that was part of his plan all along. Though I am disappointed he didn't pick me up at the airport himself, I understand now why he didn't. This was meant to be a surprise and our welcome home to each other.

"Look at me, pet," Caden commands and I raise my eyes to his. His eyes are warm, approving and there is something burning there. Love, lust, devotion maybe? I've gotten so good at reading him, but tonight he's hiding something. "I have a present for you. Close your eyes."

I do as requested but keep my face pointed upward. I hear him lower himself back to his knees then he brushes a gentle finger over my collar bone, toward my neck. His hand grasps the chain he'd given me before he'd left.

Caden wanted to tie himself to me, show me that I truly belong to him so he'd given me a necklace that was quite masculine and yet very Caden. It's a black chain link that comes to rest at the middle of my sternum, over my heart. The links are small and the necklace fits well under clothing or over it, depending on the day or clothing choice. I prefer it under my clothes so that I can feel it against my

skin and let it remind me of him every time it moves. When he'd clasped it around my neck he'd told me that it was my training collar, but I got the impression it was something more. It was put there to remind me that I belong to him and no one else. He'd also said it was a gentle reminder to him that I was truly his.

He removes the chain from my neck and a small whimper escapes my lips.

"Relax, sweet boy." I try, but it's hard. I hadn't realized the effect of the collar on my psyche until he tried to remove it. I've never taken it off. I wore it constantly. I feel his hands slide around my neck and something cool presses against my skin. "In here, you will trade your everyday collar for this one." He clasps the new collar around my neck and immediately warmth returns to my body.

"Thank you, Master," I tell him with a whisper.

Once he has it clasped around my neck, his hand comes to my cheek, his fingers slide into my hair. "Anytime, sweet boy." I lean into his touch. The warmth of his fingers and the security of my new collar send waves of desire through me. I haven't felt this way in so long. It's overwhelming me slightly. The anticipation of what he plans to do to me tonight sends a shiver through me. "What is it, pet?" he asks. His tone is commanding but gentle.

"I'm just excited, Master."

"For what?" he asks.

"For whatever Master has planned for tonight. And..." I pause, pulling in a ragged breath.

"And?"

"And I'm happy you're home," I breathe.

"Stand," he orders softly.

I do as he asks; his hand never leaves my cheek as I do.

"Open your eyes, boy," he tells me and I do, finding his immediately. They're warm, adoring me. "So am I," he breathes before sealing his lips over mine.

Caden

I release Aryn from our kiss. "Are you ready?" I ask him.

He nods.

"Good," I say and I slide my hand down his body, brushing over the black leather collar I've given him. It's not a training collar, it's my collar, his collar. But we will get to that a little later. For now, I need him under my control. "It's my goal to make you soar tonight, sweet slut. Are you ready to soar?"

He trembles. "Yes, Master."

My fingers continue trailing down his chest and over his abs before grabbing hold of his cock. His eyes roll around in his skull at my touch. "Easy boy, or I will cage him."

His eyes widen momentarily. "Cage him?" he asks.

I raise an eyebrow at him.

"I'm sorry, Master. What do you mean by 'cage him'?

My lips twitch in approval at his backpedaling. We've not been able to play like this in a long time, but he's doing a beautiful job of giving me everything I'd hoped for out of tonight and then some. I grip his cock and walk toward the dresser. He groans and follows behind me as I lead him where I want him to go by his cock.

The power slides through me and my sense of Domspace threatens to overpower me. He's already given me so much tonight and we've barely gotten started. Once we're standing in front of the dresser I look at him, his cock twitches in my hand. "Open the top drawer," I tell him and he obliges.

He pulls a breath through his teeth at what's laid out on the black velvet lining the drawer. There are three different kinds of cages. Stages of training. The first is made of silicone. Not entirely designed to inflict pain, but still designed to stop an erection from forming.

The second is a metal one, similar in shape to the silicone one. This one, though metal, is lined with silicone, still preventing an erection from forming but not entirely painful. The last one is the one I hope to one day use on him regularly. It's made of only metal and will cause pain if he starts to get an erection. "Remember how I told you that all your orgasms belong to me?"

He shivers. "Yes, Master."

"These will prevent this." I squeeze his cock in my hand to emphasize my point. His eyes rattle around again, the pleasure of my squeeze is proving to drive him crazy, which is the point. "From getting hard."

He shivers, this time harder, and his eyes dart to mine. "Why would you not want me to be hard, Master?"

I give him a wicked little grin. "Because, pet, there are times when I want to play with you and deny you at the same time. There will be times, mostly in punishing circumstances, where I want you to stay soft so that you remember where you belong. And," I pause and give him a pointed look. His eyes are a little wild with fear. "I want you to be able to control your erection."

He nods in understanding. "Yes, Master." His voice is barely above a whisper.

"But we will get into that another time. The three different cages you see are designed for training. Understand?"

"Yes, Master."

I smile "Good. Close the drawer," I tell him before I set his everyday training collar on the dresser before leading him toward the cross. We're standing before it and I snap my fingers. It's his command to kneel.

He does so without a second of thought. He places his hands on his thighs palms up as he lowers his head to the floor.

"You please me so, sweet boy," I coo as I slide my hand into his hair. With my free hand, I unbutton my jeans before pushing them down enough to free my cock. "Take it," I order. This time a little harsher and he reaches his hand up, blindly wrapping his hand around my cock. Pleasure sky rockets through me the moment his warm hand wraps around my throbbing shaft. "Suck it, slut." I demand and he doesn't hesitate.

His head comes up, his mouth opens, his tongue darts out and he places the head of my cock against the warm, wetness of his tongue before sucking me into his mouth. I hiss through my teeth as he gently scrapes his teeth along my shaft. I roughly fist his hair between my fingers. He stills. "Look at me," I command.

His eyes come to mine, my cock still buried in his mouth. I simply shake my head and he nods slightly. I slide my other hand into his hair, holding on to him as I slide my cock in and out his mouth while holding his head still.

My need to come soars higher the longer I pump in and out of his mouth. He knows I'm punishing him and he whimpers around my cock. "Take it, my sweet slut. Take it all," I groan and he moans around my shaft as I continue to pump in and out of him.

I don't stop until I feel my balls tighten and my orgasm rages through my shaft. I grunt out my orgasm along his tongue and he swallows down every drop as I rub the rest of my orgasm from my cock.

I release my hands from his hair, but not before giving him a gentle touch of approval on his chin, forcing his face up to mine. I give him a satisfied smile. "Thank you, pet," I tell him and he smiles. His eyes are a little glossy and I know what I'm doing is working. "Stand for me, facing the cross," I direct him. He stands and faces the cross in front of him. I lean into his ear. "You please me, sweet boy." He shudders and I smile before adding, "Step up to it." He spreads his legs and places his hands over the top of the cross.

I step in close and press my warm body against his. My cock is already returning to its previous hardness as it presses against him. He shivers, but says nothing as I lock one wrist into the restraints at the top.

I let my hard cock slide across his backside as I move to the other arm. I secure that one to the cross and let my hand trail down his arm. My touch leaves goosebumps in its wake and Aryn's breathing hitches in his throat.

I let my hand slide all the way down his side, over his hip and down his thigh as I lower myself to the a kneeling position to secure his left ankle to the cross. I repeat the trailing process back up his leg and up between his cheeks, touching the puckered rim of his as and he hisses. I watch his cock jump and a little trail of pre-cum leaks from the tip. I smile before moving my hand to the other cheek and down his other leg before securing it to the cross like the other.

He does exactly as I expect him to. He tests his bonds. I smile because he knows he's secure, but he needs that satisfaction of knowing he's not going anywhere to get into the scene.

I use a firm grip in his hair to turn his head toward mine. His eyes are glossy and hooded when I press my lips to his. He moans into my mouth and I swallow it. Soaking up his submission and his desire. I pull my mouth from his. "What's your safeword, pet?" I ask him.

"Hollywood, Master."

"What do you say when you're unsure?" I ask him.

"Yellow, Master."

"Where are you right now, pet?"

"Green, Master."

"Good," I respond before releasing his hair from my hand. I let my hand trail down his neck and over his back until I find the soft globe of his ass. I rub my hand around it gently before pulling back and giving it a firm smack. He jumps slightly.

"Where are you right now, pet?"

"Green, Master. Still green," he moans.

I smile again before repeating the process on his other cheek. Smacking it once, then spanking his other cheek and back to the left one.

"And now, my pet?"

"Green, Master." His voice grows a little huskier with each answer.

A shiver of anticipation slides through me as I spank each cheek again, each time a little harder than the previous. This time he doesn't jump, but I hear his hiss as he processes the pain.

"Pet?"

"Green, Master."

I gently rub my hands along his pink cheeks and then slide around the front of the cross. I'm standing face to face with him. "Open your eyes, slut."

It takes him a moment to do so and when he does, his eyes are hooded and glossy. I grab his cock, he moans and closes his eyes. I give his cock a firm squeeze. "Open your eyes," I order and he does. "Keep them open," I tell him and he nods slightly.

"Sorry, Master."

"Feels good, doesn't it, slut?"

"Yes, Master, very good. I've missed you, Master," he moans.

I lower myself to my knees before him. Because of the cross, he can't see me, but he can certainly feel me when I wrap my mouth around the head of his cock. He cries out in response. His body trembles and his bonds shake against the cross. "Do you want to come, slut?"

"Yes, Master," he groans. "Please, Master."

"No," I order and he sighs.

"Yes, Master," he mutters.

I smile in satisfaction before taking his cock back into my mouth. I let my tongue swirl around the head and I'm rewarded with a sweet drop of his cum and I moan around his cock. I missed this, missed his taste, his smell, and most importantly, him.

I warred with myself about how to do this tonight. A part of me

wanted to just drag him to bed and make love to him all night long, but a larger part needed this. Needed him at my mercy.

I continue sucking his shaft and his grunts and moans grow more and more desperate. His body trembles. I cup his balls in my hand and he cries out, "Please, Master, I can't..." He hisses through his teeth as I tighten my grip on his balls and suck his cock harder into my mouth. "Oh god, please Master Caden, please, I can't take it anymore. Please let me come."

I smile around his shaft before releasing his cock. "Come, sweet boy, come now," I demand and suck his cock back into my mouth, this time harder and more forceful as he explodes down my throat. I swallow every drop, swirling my tongue around the head of his cock. He twitches against the cross and his cock softens slightly. I smile as I release him and pull a silicone ring from my back pocket.

I stretch it before slipping it over the head of his cock, and bringing it down to the base. "Oh, God," he cries out when the ring tightens around his shaft. His cock hardens further. "Thank you, Master," he moans.

I give him an evil smirk before sucking his cock back into my mouth.

"Oh fuck," he cries above me and I nip the head of his cock with my teeth. "I'm sorry, Master." His voice is full of emotion and apology now.

I gently lavish his cock for a few more seconds before releasing him completely and standing up. Our noses mere inches apart from each other. I brush my nose against his. "You please me, pet. Now, are you ready to soar?"

"Yes, Master," he moans and I step away from him entirely.

CHAPTER TWENTY-ONE
Caden

*A*ryn shivers at the loss of contact with me before I move away. I pull down a couple floggers and what I'm hoping will be the finishing touch on tonight. I set them on a table near the cross before heading back to the dresser we were at a few moments ago. I pull open the third drawer and pull out a couple of things before returning to Aryn.

I shuck off my pants, leaving me naked. My cock is hard as stone, my desire for him spikes hotter with each passing minute. This is going to be equally as hard - no pun intended - for him as it is for me. It's taking every ounce of control I have not to untie him and bend him over the spanking bench. I shudder as the visual consumes me before I manage to shake it off. I grab the two things I'd pulled from the drawer and I shake one of them. Once I'm satisfied with it, I pop the cap and watch him squirm against the cross.

I squirt some lube over the plug I selected from the drawer. It's not as big as I am, but Aryn and I have already completed his training in that area so I know this won't be difficult for him. This particular plug vibrates and I have the controller to make it go at will. I press the button to make sure it's ready to go and Aryn shudders again at the sound the plug makes in my hand. I lube up the plug, leaving excess on my hand to help him a little more.

I press my naked body against his backside. Doing scenes naked isn't usually my style, but I don't plan on stopping to strip when this is over. Aryn melts into me and releases a sigh of satisfaction. I smile before I place my lubed up hand along the tight bud of his entrance and he shivers again. I gently work the lube on the outside before pressing a finger inside. He relaxes immediately having learned the hard way what tensing does when I'm playing back here. "Well done, pet," I console him.

"Thank you, Master." There's a vibration to his voice that lets me know he's enjoying what I'm doing to him and I smile.

I add another finger, flexing in and out of him and he moans. "Does that feel good, slut?"

"Yes, Master," he moans.

"Good," I murmur as I click on the plug.

I smile when he shivers again before pushing his ass out slightly. I want to smack him for his eagerness, but my hands are full.

I remove my hand, taking the plug from my other hand before pressing it against his entrance. He moans as I push it inside of him. "That's it, pet. Feel it, savor it. Simmer for me, pet," I encourage him. His breathing is ragged as I push the plug in farther, drawing it closer to the widest part of the plug. I pull the plug back slightly, giving the lube on the plug a chance to coat him before pushing it in farther. He moans a little louder as the widest point pushes past the tight ring of muscle.

The gentle vibration continues and he jerks slightly. "Oh, God," he moans and I turn the plug off. He whimpers. I pull away from him, pressing the button on the remote, sending the plug vibrating again and he shakes in his bindings.

Satisfied, I let the plug go for a few moments while I wipe my hands on a towel, cleaning the lube from them before picking up one of the lighter floggers. Once I'm ready to go, I turn off the vibration on the plug. I want him to feel this, savor it.

Over the course of the last six months, Aryn and I have worked with floggers, crops and tested a cane, which was not something he enjoyed. I can understand it, but it will be an effective punishment tool, given that pain seems to be something he's enjoying. Eventually the cane won't be so effective on him, but until then, I've got a tool in my arsenal.

Stepping up to him, I trail the falls of the flogger up his legs, over his ass and across his back. "Breathe, pet," I remind him and I hear an intake of air and I smile. Once I've covered every inch of his backside with the flogger falls, I step back, giving myself some room

before I start to swing it softly against his backside.

After a few strokes, Aryn's head lulls forward and I know he's sliding into his happy place. I build up slowly to harder and heavier strikes. One particular strike causes his head to come up and a growl to split his lips. I stop, pressing myself against him, sliding my hand into his hair. "Breathe through it, my sweet little slut," I groan and I hear him steady his breathing. "Where are you, pet?"

"Green, Master."

I pull his head back, turning it slightly to claim his mouth as I press my body harder into his. He moans as I slide my tongue in along his. "Good boy," I murmur in his ear before stepping back. I go back to swinging the flogger with the same intensity as before. It takes just a couple of strokes before his head lulls forward again.

I don't stop swinging the flogger a little harder and a little slower than before, allowing him some time to process the sensations radiating through his body.

I'm hitting him all up and down his backside, occasionally across the backs of his thighs. I can tell when a fall strikes his sack because he'll grunt and hiss through his teeth but he is processing quickly.

I stop and move to press myself against him. He moans as my warmth consumes him and I slide my hand along his warm backside. The strikes have caused the blood to rush to the surface, warming him and I take comfort from that. "More for my sweet boy?"

"Please, Master," he mutters and I know he's starting to float.

I step away from him and grab the other flogger. As I make my way back to him, I swing both at the same time. Both floggers are very different in their sensations, which was what I wanted him to feel. The first was softer, thuddier. The second one is more sharp and stingy. I want him to experience both.

I slowly strike his back, first with the softer, then with the sharper. He rattles his bindings after the first hit, but I don't give him much time to think before the second strike of the softer, then the harder.

Alternating between the two sensations sends Ayrn's body into overdrive. His arms go limp against the cross and he settles into the support of his bindings. He's soaring with each stroke against his back.

I pull in a deep breath, drawing strength from him, and I begin to find my own happy place with each stroke. Taking his submission, cradling it and devouring it with each stroke, each pass.

I gradually increase the speed and strength behind each pass and he's processing, his body is limp and sated as I do so.

After a couple minutes, I pause, pressing myself against him. His entire upper torso is warm against me. His body hums, his breathing is even and shallow. If I didn't know any better, I could almost assume he's asleep, but this is Aryn's space.

I place both floggers in my left hand before running my right up and down his back, letting my hand comfort him before I slide it into his hair, tugging hard on the strands between my fingers. He whimpers. "Where are we, sweet boy?"

A little smile plays on his lips. "Green, Master," he moans.

I kiss him again. This time more urgent and desperate. He groans into my mouth and I smile against his lips. "Greedy little minx," I tease as I pull away.

"Only for you, Master," he murmurs.

"Better be," I retort and step away from him, releasing his hair as I go.

I put the floggers on the table before grabbing a black leather single tail whip and returning to him.

Aryn

I feel Caden's warmth close to me as he returns. I vaguely heard him set the floggers on the table, but I'm pretty certain he's not done with me. The idea sends a shiver through me while at the same time I feel something thin and light against my leg moving up my body. It's not a flogger or even the cane - thank God - but it's light and tickles slightly. I fight the urge to let the tickle consume me as he brings it up along my leg, over my ass cheek and then over my back. Once he reaches my shoulder, the air shifts just before the object lands gently on my shoulder, sliding down and off only to return again and again. The light touch quickly turns harder as he moves down my back.

I can't quite make out what it is he's holding but I shiver in anticipation of what he's going to do.

Gently I feel the kiss of the object as he moves along my backside. Each touch kissing my flesh a little harder.

I moan.

The slight kiss of pain sending me higher with each little stroke. Each little kiss makes my body come alive and shivers slide throughout my limbs. Caden steps back further and further but the motion never stops. Each flick gets further apart.

"Where are we, sweet boy?" I hear him ask me.

It takes a moment for my brain and mouth to come back together, "green, Master."

Each lick of what he has in his hand starts to intensify against my ass cheeks. Each flick a harder kiss than before. Each one causing a flicker of pain that radiates throughout my body as I process each strike.

Then I hear a slight pop and a lick of fire races up my backside, followed by a softer flick. I groan. I want more. "Please, Master," I

moan without thinking.

"What, sweet boy?"

"More," I moan.

Another pop, followed by a hotter lick of fire and I cry out.

"Where are we, boy?" he says harshly.

"Green," I cry out.

Then another pop, this time the fire burns and simmers just on the surface, then I'm met with a really loud pop and the burn explodes across my flesh. Tears drop from my eyes and I cry out.

At the same time, it's like I leave my body, floating higher and higher with each little flick, each pop and each stroke of the whip my Master yields over me.

He doesn't stop. The pops come more frequently and the fire ignites my flesh with each kiss of the tail. My body is a live wire, my whole being is alive in a sensation unlike anything I've ever felt before.

My knees give out as I give into the cross.

My mind is foggier, sounds meld into sensation, sensations overwhelm me.

My cock twitches, burns, my balls tighten and my orgasm roars despite the cock ring around my shaft. The force is so powerful that I can no longer hold myself up. The cross takes my weight and my orgasm explodes out of me and Caden is pressed against me, holding me, murmuring sweet words to me. Tears stream down my face.

The next thing I know, my hands and legs are free of the cross and I'm curled up in Caden's arms.

I feel his gentle lips against my cheeks as he soaks up my tears with whispers of encouragement, endearments I've never heard him speak before. "I love you, my dear sweet boy," he breathes against my lips and I melt into him. Wrapping my arms around his neck, trying desperately to get closer to him.

He cups my face between his palms before pressing his lips to mine. My heart explodes, full of love, devotion and an undeniable feeling of completeness as Caden takes me to the bed in his playroom. He lays me on my stomach gently. Then he pulls the plug from within before he climbs behind me. I feel his hands on my hips, lifting me. I follow his lead and settle on my knees.

I whimper, "Please, Caden. I need you." I cry out as his cock press into me. My heart roars in my chest. Love, desire and need explode the moment he bottoms out inside me. His hand glides up and down my back before both hands take hold of my hips as he thrusts in and out of me. My cock is rock hard beneath me. I want so desperately to grab hold of it, to come with him, but I behave myself.

"Grab it, sweet boy, stroke it for me," he orders as if reading my mind and my mind explodes with undeniable pleasure the moment my hand wraps around my cock.

It takes me about three strokes and I'm the edge. He thrusts into me, harder and faster. "Aryn, oh God," he moans above me. "Come for me, Aryn," he cries above me and I stroke my cock harder before I explode all over the bed as I feel Caden pour himself inside me.

"I love you," I cry out with my orgasm.

CHAPTER TWENTY-TWO
Aryn

I can't bring myself to open my eyes.

I'm wrapped in Caden's warmth. His arm is wrapped around my stomach, his other arm is under my head and his leg is hitched over mine. I can feel his gentle, shallow breathes against my back and his erection pressed between us. I smile as the memories of last night come flooding back to me.

My submission.

Caden's command and control over me and my body.

Caden consuming me in a way he's never done before.

My breathing stops when I remember the three little words that were finally spoken between us.

We've been together for six months and in those six months I fell wholly and completely in love with him but the idea of saying those three words scared the hell out of me.

I learned so much more about him and Michelle, about what their relationship was like and it should have made me feel concern for us, but it didn't. In fact it had the opposite effect. I realized that while he loved Michelle immensely, he was open to loving me just the same and last night he finally said it. Finally admitted it.

A warmth spreads through me. It's a comfortable warmth, a safe and secure warmth from the idea that Caden has opened up to me in a way that six months ago I could have only hoped for.

I turn in his arms and pain shoots from my backside when I do. I hiss and moan through my teeth at the same time.

"Is it bad?"

Sleepy eyes meet mine and I stare into his seeing the same mysterious look that I'd noticed last night looking back at me. I shake my head. "No, Master."

A smile spread across his lips before he leans in and presses them to mine. "Good, and formalities are over," he tells me. I smile wide before rolling into him further. I ignore the pain radiating across my ass from the whip last night and press him back into the mattress.

"Say it again," I breathe as I hover over him.

"Formalities are..." I cut him off with a shake of my head.

"The other thing." I give him a smirk.

He narrows his eyes in thought then reality dawns and his eyes light up. He wraps his arms around me, holding my chest to his with his lips mere inches away from my own. I shiver. "I love you, Aryn Becker," he breathes and I slam my lips against his. Stealing his breath away as he squeezes tighter. Our lips dance and move as one before I flick his upper lip, hoping he'll catch my drift and open for me. He does and I slide my tongue in along his at the same time he flicks his hips into mine. I moan and release his lips before pressing my forehead against his.

"I love you," I breathe back at him.

His hips thrust up again and I smile before kissing him chastely on the lips. I move down to his jaw, along his neck to that sweet spot between his neck and shoulder where I kiss and flick my tongue. I move farther down his chest, sliding my body down his smooth, muscular frame. His cock gets trapped against my chest as I kiss and lick my way from one nipple to the other.

He slides his hand into my hair and I smile as I kiss and lick my way lower until I find a spot just below the V in his abdomen and I kiss it. His breathing hitches and I flick my tongue against the same spot and he shudders beneath me. I smile wider before flicking my tongue across the underside of his cock. My eyes meeting his as I do.

He has a beautiful smile on his face that melts my insides. "I missed this," I breathe. My cool breath causes him to shiver as it passes over his cock and the wet trail I left on it.

"Me too, sweet boy. Me too."

Despite the lack of formalities, Caden has always called me that term. It's usually when he uses 'sweet slut' or 'slut' that I instantly pool into submission, but sweet boy sends my heart soaring.

In another heartbeat, I'm back to lavishing his cock with a fat tongue. He groans as he closes his eyes and his hand loosens in my hair before coming to rest on the side of my face. With a gentle nudge he coaxes me back up to his lips. I crawl up his body to find his lips ready for me and I take them slow, passionate kiss.

His hand slides from my hair and down my back but he stops at the small of my back before the crest of my cheeks. He pulls back slightly and I let my breathing return to normal. "I'm so proud of you," he breathes and my heart swells with pride.

I cock my head at him. "For what?" I ask.

"Last night. You were stunning and beautiful. You put all your trust in me to take you to a place you wanted to be." I blush at his words. "I love making you do that." His thumb rubs along my pink cheekbone and I smile before grabbing his hand and bringing his palm to my lips and kissing it. His other hand moves off my back and comes up to cup my face. He looks me square in the eyes and says, "I need to feel you." I nod my understanding. I raise myself off him and reach for the nightstand where I pull out a bottle of lube and he smiles. I set it next to him before kissing my way back down his body.

I suck his cock back into my mouth while I reach for the lube I pulled from the nightstand. I tease his cock while I pour some into my hand before closing the cap. I press my hands together, spreading the lube between them. When I'm ready, I release his cock and he lifts for me. With my left hand I grab my cock and start stroking up and down, coating my cock and with my right, I slowly start to play with his back entrance. He groans when I make contact and his breathing hitches when I press a finger inside.

"So tight," I breathe and he smiles.

Don't let his softness fool you. Caden is still very much in control,

I remind myself. I slip another finger inside and he arches his back. "I love your fingers," he murmurs and I smile before I slip a third finger inside, stretching him to accommodate my girth and he writhes on the bed.

Satisfied that I've worked him up enough, I pull my fingers back before I line the head of my cock up with his entrance and press inside. His head lulls to the side and his eyes close, savoring the feel of me spreading him open.

I push the head of my cock past the tight ring and I tremble with a moan. I adjust his legs, putting his feet on my shoulders, lifting him slightly to allow me more access and he comes with me willingly. I push in farther, his muscles contract and I groan. "So tight," I groan before pushing in until my pubic bone presses against his ass cheeks. I sit for a moment, allowing him a chance to get used to my invasion and then I start to move, slowly at first.

His eyes meet mine and I see the same mysterious look as before and I finally realize what it is. It's love. He loves me and I love him.

With my left hand, the one with some lube remaining on it, I grab his cock, stroking it in time with my thrusts.

"Oh, fuck," he growls and his eyes roll up. "Don't stop."

I don't stop.

I push in and pull out, each pass getting harder and faster as I claim him in the same manor he claimed me last night.

Each thrust is met with a tug of his cock.

I feel my orgasm building, but I need him with me. I stroke his cock harder and faster than my thrusts inside and he comes apart beneath me. Incoherent grunts, groans and moans meet my ears with the tiny flexes of his muscles as he milks my cock.

"Don't stop," he cries out and I speed up, drawing closer to my own orgasm. His cock twitches, hardens and explodes in my hand as Caden calls out my name with his orgasm.

I thrust twice inside him and pour all of myself inside him. Taking him, loving him. I release his cock and lower his legs; my cock is still inside but softening as I lean down and take his mouth with mine.

We lie in silence while our breathing returns to normal and both our cocks soften. I soon get off him and go into the bathroom. I clean myself up and before I can bring him a warm washcloth to do the same, he joins me in the bathroom.

He nods toward me. "Have you looked?" he asks. I narrow my eyes in question, he smiles wide. "At your ass, baby," he chuckles.

"Oh," I say and shake my head.

"Look," he tells me and I turn around, putting my ass to the mirror so I can see.

"Holy shit," I say breathlessly as I take in the red angry lines across my ass. "Huh?" I say.

"What?" he asks.

"It didn't feel like it hurt at all," I tell him and he gives me a knowing smirk.

"Pain is all in your head. How we handle it and what it feels like. I warmed you up for the sole purpose of using the whip on you last night," he explains with a hint of mischief in his voice.

"I think it helped that I had no idea what it was at first. Not until the popping started. By that point I was floating so high I'm not sure there would have been much to bring me down," I tell him honestly.

He gives me his knowing smirk again. "That was the idea." He wraps his arms around me, holding me to his chest.

"I was coming to clean you up," I whisper in his ear.

"I have a better idea," he replies and he looks over at the tub. "Besides, it will help." His hand gently touches my ass and I hiss slightly. "When we're done, I'll rub some more arnica cream on it."

I vaguely remember him rubbing something on me last night; it must be the same stuff. He takes my hand and leads me to the tub where he fires it up and the tub fills with warm swirling water.

CHAPTER TWENTY-THREE
Caden

*A*ryn sits between my legs as I gently wash his chest with the bath sponge as he rests his head on my shoulder. "How are you feeling?" he asks me.

I smile. "I'm tired, but I'll be alright. I just need to stay out of bed for the day and I'll be able to slip back to normal," I tell him. I won't lie; the jet lag is hitting me pretty hard.

"I remember coming back from Australia. I was a log for four days and I was only gone for a few of those days," he tells me.

"Yeah, I imagine it's gonna hit me worse in a day or two," I tell him.

"When do you have to go back?" I hear the sadness in his question. I expected it, but it still makes me sad that he thinks I'm going to have to leave again.

"I don't, well, at least not for overseas. I need to be in Los Angeles a week from tomorrow."

Today is Saturday and I'd had every intention of taking Aryn to The Box tonight, but I'm not sure if we're going to make it. Least of all, if we go I'm going to want to scene with him and I'm not sure he's up to that again so soon after last night. I got him pretty good with the whip and when he sat in the water I could tell he is in more pain than he's admitting. I should punish him for his lack of honesty, but in reality, when he's not thinking about it, I'm sure it doesn't hurt that much. "What about you?" I ask him.

"I'm good to go back whenever. Our schedule is really light for a couple months, but I'm free for at least the next week."

"Good." I squeeze him a little tighter.

He gets quiet and I can tell he's thinking about something. I don't want to press, but we've not seen each other in two months and the silence is deafening. "Talk to me?" I ask rather than tell him.

He shifts to look at me. "I'm just enjoying this. I missed this."

"I missed it too, lover, but I can tell there are wheels turning in that brain of yours."

He gives me a humorless laugh, but he sighs and starts talking. "Honestly, I'm not sure it's relevant anymore," he breathes.

"Everything that goes on in that brain of yours is relevant, love," I reassure him. "I want to know everything you're thinking about, regardless of what it is."

He sighs again and he shifts, turning around to look at me. "Honestly?"

"Always, Aryn. You know that."

He frowns. "I do." He nods his head. "I just, up until last night, I was worried about this." He gestures between us. "About where we're going with this." He sighs and cast his eyes downward. "Up until last night and again this morning, I wasn't..." he pauses.

"You weren't sure how I felt about you?" I ask. He nods. "Because I hadn't said it?" I ask him and he nods again. I drop the sponge and reach out to tuck my fingers under his chin, lifting his face to look at me. Slowly he responds to my coaxing. "Aryn, there is nothing in this world that I want more than you."

He gives me a small, sad smile. "I think I just needed to hear it. To feel it. You being gone has left me feeling so lonely, that I..."

I cut him off, "Why didn't you tell me?"

His eyes narrow at me. "Tell you what?"

"That you were feeling lonely."

"I..." he stutters. "I didn't want to worry you. I didn't want you to worry because there was nothing you could do about it. Because I felt foolish for feeling that way, because I had no business questioning how you felt about me and yet I was."

"Oh, baby, I'm sorry you felt that way. If I'd known I'd have..."

"You weren't exactly in a position to come home, Cay." I smile at

his nickname for me.

"No, I wasn't, but I would have tried harder to make contact with you more. Had Dex and Raine..."

He shakes his head. "I wasn't missing a friend, Cay, I was missing you, my boyfriend, my lover." He blushes and adds, "My Master."

"I'm sorry, baby," I tell him and pull him toward me. He comes willingly and I wrap my arms around him.

"I know you have a job to do, so when I felt lonely, I felt selfish and it didn't make me feel very good."

I smile into his hair. "Sometimes you have a right to be selfish. I'm sorry I didn't see it."

"It's okay," he tells me softly. "I guess I needed to hear you say it more than I realized. I wanted to know where we were going and talking about it over the phone didn't exactly seem appropriate, so I bottled it up. It's my fault."

I hug him a little tighter. "A little, yes. But I understand not wanting to talk about it over the phone. That's why I never said it until last night," I tell him and it's true. I realized quite a while ago I was falling in love with Aryn, but at the same time it scared the hell out of me. "For the longest time, I was afraid loving you meant I was letting Shelly go." I admit.

He pulls free of my grasp to look at me. "You know that's not what I want..." I press my finger to his lips, silencing him.

"I know that's not what you intended, but I also know that just because I love you, it doesn't mean I don't still love Shelly, it just means I love her a little differently. She's gone. I can't have her anymore, but you're here and I have you and I will not do anything to jeopardize that. Not now, not ever."

He nods his understanding with a smile before he leans forward and presses his lips to mine before pulling away. "So I guess maybe now isn't the best time to tell you what else has been bothering me?"

"If it's bothering you, then it is the best time," I tell him sternly.

He takes a deep breath. "What would you do or say if I told you that I want kids?" he asks and I stiffen, my eyes locking on his. He continues, "I know about Shelly, I know…" Again, I place my finger over his lips to hush him before dropping my hand and balancing the collar around his neck over my fingers.

"What if I told you that the collar I placed on you last night wasn't a training collar, at least not in my mind it wasn't."

His eyes widen in shock.

"What if I also told you that I fully intend to collar you before this week is out?"

His eyes shimmer with unshed tears. I know in that moment that I've reached the very deepest part of his submissive self and I place my hand against his cheek. "I'm in this, Aryn. For the long haul. From today, tomorrow, next week, month, year, forever." I breathe the last word. "If you want kids, then we will find a way to make that happen."

A tear escapes his eye. "But I want you to want them, too."

I smile at him. "I've always wanted children, Aryn. It's one of the many things I've struggled with over the last couple of months. I was scared because you and I simply can't do it. We need a third party involved, whether it's a surrogate or an adoption agency." My voice drops a little lower. "When I realized that you and I can't do it, I questioned what it is that we're doing together, but then when the idea of losing you hit me, I thought my world had completely exploded around me. I couldn't breathe." Another tear falls from his eye and I swipe it away with my thumb. "It was then that I had my answer. Submission, marriage, collar, family, all of it. I want it all, Aryn, and I don't want it with anyone but you." I punctuate my point by slamming my lips against his.

The emotions overwhelm him and he melts into my kiss and my touch as a couple more tears slide down his face.

He pulls back. "I don't know why I'm crying."

I smile at him, "I do. Subspace is a very powerful thing. It's just you coming down off the adrenaline rush. It will pass," I tell him and it's true.

"I think it's more than that," he says softly. "I think it has everything to do with the fact that I'm so happy right now."

I chuckle, "There's that too, love."

Aryn and I sat there in companionable silence for a while before we decided to get out. I helped him dry off and then led him to the bed where I spread arnica cream over his backside. His hissed and groaned a couple of time, but in the end he seemed to be feeling better. "It's just a reminder of where you belong," I told him.

He looked at me with a smile on his face and replied, "I'll never forget where I belong, Master."

My attempt at staying awake for the day failed miserably. Jet lag started to set in and Aryn knew it so he put me to bed. We cuddled for a while before I dozed off.

A ringing phone, not my phone, pulls me from my slumber and my eyes open. Aryn is sleeping next to me and he starts to stir. "Your phone, babe," I tell him and he reaches for his phone on the nightstand. He stiffens when he looks at it

"Crap," he snaps before bringing it to his ear. "What is it, Alyce?"

"Alyce?" I whisper, and he pulls the phone down and mouths, 'my sister'.

I can't hear Alyce's side of the conversation but I'm watching Aryn very carefully as his face pales, going ashen at the words he's hearing on the other end of the line.

"When?" he asks before falling silent again. "Yeah, I'll be there." Another pause and my heart starts racing in my chest. "I'll be there by the end of the day," he says softly into the phone. "Love you too, Alyce."

he slowly pulls his phone away from his ear and hits the red button. "I have to go," he breathes.

"Where are we going, Aryn?" I ask him, using a slightly more commanding tone. From the look of shock on his face, I think he needs it.

His eyes meet mine. "Billings, my mom's dead," he tells me deadpan.

I nod. "I'll make the arrangements," I tell him as I climb out of bed. I go to the closet and find a pair a flannel pants and grab Aryn a pair of sweats and return to the bed. He hasn't moved.

I climb onto the bed, getting close to his face. "Look at me," I command and his eyes move to mine. "Are you alright?" I ask. He nods slightly. "Talk to me, Aryn," I urge.

He shakes his head. "I knew she was sick and I didn't care," he confesses in a soft voice.

"She didn't deserve your worry," I remind him. He told me all about the things his mother did in the past and about her husband, Jason. Not to mention his brother Alyx. But Alyce, that's another story.

"I shouldn't go home," he tells me.

"You should, it sounds like Alyce needs you," I say to him softly.

He nods. "She's a mess." The light returns to his eyes and he returns to me in the here and now.

"There's my sweet boy."

He gives me a small grin. "I had no idea the news would hit me so hard."

"We never know how things are going to hit us until they actually do. So, let's get some arrangements made and we will be on our way, okay?"

"You just got home, you don't need..."

I place my finger over his lips and shush him. "No arguments,

Aryn. You need me, so I will be there."

He nods and after a beat he whispers, "Thank you."

"We're in this together, every step of the way, Aryn. Get me?"

He smiles a real smile and replies, "I get you."

"Good, grab what you need from the closet, what you don't have here we will get when we get there. I'm also calling Dex."

"No, don't."

I shake my head. "He's your best friend. You need him."

Aryn just nods before he climbs off the bed and puts on the pants I brought him before he disappears into the closet to grab a suitcase and pull some things together.

I reach for my phone on the nightstand and open it, finding Dex's number. I call Aryn's best friend.

"Hey, man. Welcome home," Dex greets me after a couple rings.

"Thanks, brother. Though I wish I was calling on better terms."

"What happened? Beck alright?"

I smile into the phone. My man and Dex are close. I'm glad they both have that. "As good as can be expected. He just got an unexpected call from his sister."

"What happened?" Dex asks.

"His mom's passed away."

"Shit," Dex snaps into the phone. "Where?"

"Billings, Montana."

"A'ight, we're on it. I'll call the rest of the..."

"Is that necessary?" I interrupt him.

"We're all family."

I nod into the phone. "Do it then. I'm calling to make arrangements now."

"We can have Cami send…"

"No, don't worry about that. I've got it covered here. Listen, can you handle hotel arrangements, or have Raine? I don't know how many rooms we'll need."

"Absolutely. We'll email you the details as soon as we have them."

"Perfect, thanks, man."

"You want me to call Derek?" he asks.

"Nope, that's my next call and our ride," I tell him into the phone.

"Perfect. We'll see you tonight."

"Thanks." Dex and I disconnect. My eyes haven't left Aryn since he went into the closet. I'm concerned about the toll this is going to take on him and it's going to be a good learning lesson for both of us.

I look back at my phone and find Derek's number and let it ring.

"Hunter," he answers the phone.

"D, it's Caden."

"Hey, man. What's going on? You back home?"

"I am, just got back yesterday."

"You in Nashville?"

"Yeah, where are you?"

"Same, we came in yesterday."

"I hate to call and ask you this, but I need a favor."

"Anything, you know that."

I nod and give the phone a sad smile as my eyes return to the closet doorway and Aryn. "Aryn just got some bad news, his mom passed away."

"Oh shit, where we going?"

I knew I could count on Derek and it's the reason I called him. "Billings."

"I'll make the calls. Want us to come too?"

"I will leave that up to you. I think Aryn can use all the support he can get right now," I tell Derek.

"You got it. I'll make the calls and text you with the details. The plane's already here, so it shouldn't take more than a couple hours, tops."

"We're packing now, so we'll be ready."

"Perfect," Derek says into the phone.

"Let Dex know you're coming, he and Raine are making hotel arrangements," I share.

"I've got room up there for you, Aryn, Dex and Raine. I'll call and have them get it set up."

"Jesus, where do you not have a house... don't answer that," I chuckle into the phone. "Thanks, man, I owe you big time."

"You owe me nothing," he says into the phone then I hear a muffled sound. "Get packed, sweetie, change of plans."

"Is she okay to travel?" I ask Derek, remembering Cotah's pregnancy.

"She's good. Commercially, maybe not so much, but we have the bedroom on the plane. If she needs to lay down, she's got somewhere to do that."

"Alright, I need to call Teddy."

"You got this, brother."

"Thanks." We terminate our call just as Aryn comes out of the closet.

He looks better than he did twenty minutes ago. "I don't have a suit here," he tells me softly.

"Don't worry about it, we'll get it taken care of. Derek is getting his plane ready and he has a house in Billings that has room for Dex, Raine, you and myself. If that's alright with you?" His eyes meet

mine then and he nods. I can tell he's still in a state of shock, but he's holding it together pretty well. "Dex is calling in the family," I tell him and he visibly relaxes and nods.

"Thank you," he tells me and I walk around the bed and wrap my arms around him.

"Anything you need, you've got it," I tell him.

He gives me a small smile. "I don't know what I'd do if you weren't here..." His voice trails off.

"I'm here," I remind him with a squeeze.

Within the hour, Aryn and I are packed and climbing into the SUV he rented at the airport. We're headed to a local airport where Derek keeps his plane when he's in town. Aryn has become a little more animated since I got off the phone with Teddy. He and Will are joining us on the plane to Billings at Derek's urging.

CHAPTER TWENTY-FOUR
Aryn

The flight was excruciatingly long and I'm not sure if it is because there's nothing I can do from up in the air, or if it is because I was trapped inside a tin can flying through the air.

Regardless, the minute my feet hit solid ground in Montana, I was in motion. Caden had arranged a car for us. Derek handled transportation for him, Teddy, Will, and Cotah. Teddy and Will will be staying with us at the house as well and that made me feel a little more comfortable. I don't know them well, but for some strange reason, I was glad they came, if for no one else but Caden.

I know he's worried about me, but he's handling me pretty well and it's a great comfort to me. Without even asking, Caden gives me the keys to the rental. "You remember your way around?" he asks.

"I think so," I tell him as we climb in.

The moment my butt hit the seat of the car, I start to freak out and Caden knows it immediately. "What is it, sweet boy?" He uses his Dom voice, therefore giving me no outlet on my answer.

"I'm embarrassed," I answer him.

He cocks his head at me and I look away from him. "Whatever for?" he asks.

"We just flew here on a private jet, we're in a fifty-thousand dollar vehicle, your house is bigger than most hotels I've stayed in, and I'm about to take you to a fucking trailer park."

"Language, pet," he snaps.

"Sorry, Master."

"You're forgiven, and under the circumstances I will allow you a lot of latitude because you deserve it, but do not forget your rules."

"I'm sorry, Master," I tell him automatically.

"You have nothing to be ashamed of, Aryn. Do you honestly think

that if I see where you grew up I'm going to think any less of the man you are today? Love you any less?"

I shake my head, it's true. "It doesn't mean I'm not embarrassed by it," I tell him softly.

"I understand that, but please understand something about me, too. I don't care where you come from, you," he gently pats my chest, right over my heart, "and this are all I care about. You could have grown up under a bridge for all I care, because all I care about is you and who you are. Not your family, not where you come from. Where you come from has shaped you into the man I love today," he tells me with such conviction that my heart swells to the point of bursting.

"Thank you, Caden," I breathe.

"That's why I'm here. Now, let's go see your sister." He smiles and I start the car.

Despite his words, the closer we get, the more anxious I become. I don't want to see Jason, and Alyx is next on my list. Alyce, on the other hand, is another story. I try and let my excitement over seeing Alyce cover everything else. Including the fact that I feel awful that my mother's death is what has brought me home for the first time in ten years.

I pull into the trailer park and Caden doesn't say a word, make a noise or even a face as we do. I have no idea what's going through his mind the closer we get, so I decide to ask, "Penny for your thoughts?"

He smiles at me. I look at him briefly before returning my eyes to the narrow roadway through the park. "just worried about you and your sister."

"Why Alyce?" I ask.

"She means a lot to you, no?"

"The world," I tell him and it's the truth.

"Then I think it's time to get her out of here. Away from Jason.

There's no telling what he's going to do now that your mother is gone."

I'd thought about the same thing on the plane. Alyce deserves so much better than this hell hole and I know she'd never leave mom, but now that mom is gone, she just might. "I was thinking the same thing. Though I don't know what to do with her exactly," I admit and it's true.

"Move her into your apartment in Los Angeles."

"I don't have room for her there," I tell him. It's true, I don't. It a perfect place for one person but more than that...realization dawns. Caden knows this.

"You do if you're not there." His voice is soft as he says it.

"Just where am I supposed to go?" I ask as I pull up in front of my old home. The place looks like shit from the outside, I shouldn't be surprised.

"I think it's time you moved in with me."

"Is that an order, Master?"

"No, just a suggestion," he says with a smile. "You asked where we go from here, right? And I told you what I wanted. Well, the first step to that is getting you and I under the same roof. So, logically, that would mean moving in with me. Let your sister sublet the apartment and you can move in with me." There's a smile tugging at the corner of his lips as he finishes.

"She'll never be able to afford that apartment," I remind him.

"Probably not, but I'm pretty sure your landlord would take a rather large check to let it slide, would he not?"

"Are you saying you're going to pay for my sister's apartment?" I ask him straight up.

"You move in with me and I will pay for whatever you need."

I sigh. "Yes, I will move in with you and we will discuss the rest later."

His tugging corners turns into a full blown smile as he reaches across the car and cups the back of my neck, pulling my lips to his in a warm, sensual kiss that sends my blood racing through my veins. All too soon he ends the kiss. "So not fair," I mutter. Caden laughs.

"You ready, pet?" His commanding tone sends warmth through me and my hand goes to the collar around my neck.

I nod. "Yes, Master."

Alyce comes flying out of the trailer the moment we get out of the car, leaping down the steps and slamming into me. Immediately she starts sobbing into my chest. "Hi, baby sis," I say softly as I wrap my arms around her, bringing my one hand to her hair, stroking it softly before kissing the top of her head.

Her light brown locks are significantly longer than the last time I saw her, but stick straight. The poor girl never had the kind of hair she could do anything with outside of a ponytail or some type of braid. We have the same brown eyes, though hers are softer and prettier, and she has the Becker chin that is square and prominent.

"I'm so happy you're here," she sobs harder and I just hold her in my arms. Caden has a soft expression on his face as he observes our greeting. He's letting me soak up the time with my sister. He no doubt saw me relax the moment she was in my arms.

After a minute or so, she pulls back, grabbing me by the biceps and peers up at me. The Montana sun is setting and the clouds are setting off a reddish glow around us. "You look amazing." She smiles.

"You're looking good yourself," I tell her and she hugs me again, this time briefly before letting me go.

"Who's this?" she asks, peering at Caden with curious eyes.

"Alyce, I'd like you to meet my boyfriend, Caden."

"Boyfriend?" Alyce says looking from me to Caden and back to me again. "Well, hot damn." She releases me and smacks her hands together. I roll my eyes as she walks over to Caden and without any warning wraps her arms around him.

Caden stands there in shock for a moment before his brain snaps to attention and he awkwardly wraps his arms around her. His eyes haven't left me and I mouth, "sorry," to him and he smiles.

"It's great to meet you, Alyce," he says.

She gives him the once over. "Why are all the gay ones the hottest ones?" Her rhetorical question sends both Caden and I laughing.

I want to say something about not always being gay, but that seems more complicated to explain. "Where's Alyx?" I ask her.

"I'm right here," Alyx says from where he's walking toward us. His eyes are narrowed on me as he's looking me over, then Caden and then finally the SUV behind us. He's tall, but not quite six foot. He's definitely put on more weight since his high school football days. The beer belly he'd already been working on when I left ten years ago is now impressive in size. His eyes were the lightest out of all of us, blue, and his hair is more blonde than brown. He's wearing clothes that embarrass me. They're dirty and it's obvious he made no effort at cleaning himself up before I arrived. Alyce had the decency to put on something nice, but Alyx? I can only shake my head. "You show up in that?"

I cock my head. "Don't fucking start, Alyx," I snap at him.

Caden's eyes narrow at me slightly as I realize I've cussed again, but I'll take my punishment.

"You can afford to show up in that and yet you couldn't send money home for your own fucking mother."

"Fuck off, Alyx, mom was not my responsibility, she was Jason's and you damn well know it. Besides, renting an SUV doesn't exactly qualify as affording a car like that."

"I've been here busting my ass for years to keep a roof over our heads and here you are, showing up in your fancy ass fucking clothes, fancy ass car. Fuck you, Aryn."

"Enough," a gravelly voice barks from the trailer. "Alyx, knock your shit off."

152

Caden raises an eyebrow at me, questioning the voice. I shrug. It's probably Jason, but he's never once defended me in anything.

"This isn't over," Alyx barks at me.

"It is over, Alyx, there ain't nothing to discuss that hasn't been said a million times before," I snap at him, ignoring the warning look from Caden at my tone. He doesn't understand my family and if I have to explain it to him to avoid punishment later on, I will.

The door to the trailer slams shut again, but I don't see anyone for a few moments until Jason rounds the corner of the trailer. He's put on some weight and he's not walking so good. "Welcome home, Aryn," Jason says cordially.

I nod to him. "Thanks," I say stoically and that's the way the night goes.

Alyce spent the next twenty minutes launching into great detail about what she's been up to these last couple of years. Everything ranging from working at a daycare center and loving it, to working on art. She was always drawing and painting whenever she could get her hands on supplies. The first Christmas after I left, I sent her a huge package of art supplies. The letter I got after Christmas contained one of her drawings that I still have to this day hanging on my wall at home.

We weren't there for an hour before I discovered that no arrangements have been made for mom and that she's being sent to the funeral home in the morning. She died in the hospital due to complications from liver cancer that spread to her lungs and then finally, her brain. Jason kept her at the hospital as long as possible so he could try and figure out how to pay for the arrangements.

I gathered that mom's treatments drained them dry even though she was on Medicare and he didn't have any money to handle the arrangements. Caden, having the massive heart that he does, offered to pay for them so I told Jason, Alyx and Alyce that Caden and I would go to the funeral home in the morning to handle everything.

As we were leaving, Alyce followed us out. "I'm really happy you're here," she whispered as she hugged me again then looked up at me, "I want to go with you tomorrow."

"Of course," I tell her. "We'll stop by and pick you up around eleven, alright?"

"Alright," she says sadly.

"You doing okay?" I ask her.

She shrugs. "As well as can be expected under the circumstances. Despite Alyx's asshole behavior earlier, he's a fucking mess and Jason isn't any better. Then again, I'm surprised he doesn't have another piece of ass in the house already."

"Alyce," I snap.

She shrugs, "You know as well as I do, when his money tree fell ill he went looking for it somewhere else. The man's a pig," she says quietly. The walls in the trailer are paper thin and there's no doubt that Jason or Alyx are listening for any piece of dirt they can get.

"I do," I breathe.

"Listen, when this is all done and over with we're going to sit down and talk," I tell her.

"About what?" she asks with a raised eyebrow.

"About moving back to Los Angeles with me," I whisper.

"Are you serious?"

I nod my head. "Later, we'll discuss it, alright?"

"I don't know if I can..."

I cut her off, "We'll discuss it, but you know as well as I do that you can and you should. Nothing good has ever come out of this trailer, it's time to move on," I tell her. She simply nods and I wrap my arm around her shoulders before kissing the top of her head. "I'll see you tomorrow," I tell her.

Caden's Command

She indicates toward Caden and tells him with a smile, "It was great meeting you, Caden."

He returns her smile, "Likewise, Alyce."

"You don't have to pay for this," Aryn argues as we drive away from the trailer.

"I know I don't, but I will," I tell him. "She may not have been the perfect mother, but she's still your mother, Aryn."

"I have enough money saved up that I can..."

"Good, keep your money, baby, please. Don't argue with me about this because I'm going to do it."

"Is this you being all Dom on me?" I snap.

Caden's eyes flash to mine. "No, Aryn, this is me taking care of the man I love. But if you'd prefer, I can use my Master tone."

Aryn visibly shudders. "No, I get it. I'm sorry, it's just..." he pauses while taking a deep breath, "Being back in that house brings up everything I've tried to suppress for the last decade."

"I understand, which is why I'm trying to make things easier for you. No reason other than that. Please believe me on that one, Aryn. I have no intention of pushing you to do something you don't want to do. If my paying for this makes you feel out of control, I will let you do it."

He sighs. "No, it's not that. It's just frustrating. Alyx crawled under my skin tonight and I just, I hate it that he blames me for being stuck here, but the reality is, I walked away. He could have walked away and he's chosen not to."

"Then let that be his problem. He can blame you all he wants, but so long as you know the reality of the situation, then that's all that matters." I place my hand on his leg. He releases the steering wheel with one hand and wraps his fingers in mine.

"I'll try," he says with promise and he pulls my hand to his lips. He gently places a kiss on the palm of my hand. "I'm glad you're here." His voice is soft, barely above a whisper.

"Me too," I respond as he drives us toward Derek's house.

It's ten to eight when we arrive outside the ranch house and there are several more cars in the lot than there should be. "Jesus, who didn't show up?" Aryn mutters.

I smile. "My guess is no one."

He shakes his head in exasperation. "This is going to be really strange."

"They're here for you," I remind him.

"I know, but it seems excessive."

"Maybe, but the bottom line is that they are your family. Maybe not Alyx, or Jason, or even your mother, but these people here, they love you so they will be here for you."

Aryn parks the SUV near the front door in between several other cars. So many in fact that I'm not sure that Billings has any more rental cars available.

Aryn and I climb out. We'd sent our luggage with Derek when we split up at the airport so we have nothing in the car to carry in with us.

I take Aryn's hand in mine as we approach the door and just as I'm about to knock the door opens and Dex is standing on the other side.

"Hi, brother," He greets Aryn before snagging him by the shoulder and pulling him in for a big ass, Dex style hug. Aryn releases my hand to return the gesture and I can tell Dex is whispering something in his ear, though I can't hear it.

"Thanks, man," Aryn says back to him and they release each other.

Dex reaches out to take my hand and pulls me into the same style hug. "Good to see you," he says. "I told him to relax, and take a deep breath," he tells me in a conspiratorial tone.

"Thanks," I whisper back. "I've been trying to tell him that for hours."

Dex laughs and releases me, "I know, man, but I gotta try."

Dex closes the door behind us. "Everyone is out on the back patio," Raine says as she comes toward Aryn.

She looks at me. "May I, Sir?" she asks.

"Of course."

She wraps her arms around Aryn's neck and pulls him into a huge hug. There are tears shimmering in her eyes. "I'm so sorry, Aryn."

"Thanks, darlin'," he drawls. "But I'm okay, really."

Oddly enough, I believe him. Given the circumstances of everything going on, he's holding it together pretty well. I'm surprised.

"Come on, let's get you two a drink," Dex says as Aryn and Raine release each other.

That's how the night goes, at least for a while.

Dex called in the calvary of friends Aryn has, including Addison, Talon, and Kyle, along with Calvin and Eric. They're the ones that hang on to Aryn the longest. Followed by some of the security guys Aryn works with, including Mills, Casey, Victoria and Rusty. All in all, there are twenty people here at the house.

Derek approaches me and asks, "How's he doing?"

"Surprisingly well," I tell him as he hands me a beer.

"That's not always a good thing," he reminds me.

"No, it's not, but I think he needs it right now. You got a room here?" I ask him.

"I do, it's not much, mostly equipment but no toys. I brought our bag with us. I thought maybe you might need it."

"I didn't even think about it," I tell him.

"I got you covered."

"Honestly, I think he's still running off of last night," I whisper. "I lit him up pretty good."

"I was wondering. I only see Cotah like that when I've fired her up. He's sitting pretty gingerly," Derek smirks.

"He took it like a champ." I smile back at him. "I'm so proud of him." Derek's smirk turns into a full blown smile. "But I won't hesitate to take him back in there if I think he needs it."

"Good, I'll have Cotah show you around later on."

"Thanks again, for everything. You'll send me a bill right?"

He snorts, "Not on your life."

I chuckle, "Figures." Good friends make the best family.

As the night progresses, I notice Aryn starts to fade fast. His endorphin rush is finally fading away and his eyes are growing heavier with each passing moment. Some of our little crowd has disbursed, headed for the hotel, but some still remain.

I talked with Teddy some and Will has been stuck to Aryn like glue tonight and I didn't realize how much he was leaning on Will for support. It warmed my heart that putting the subs together has actually paid off. Aryn is no longer afraid of his submission, nor is he afraid of his emotions, and I admire that about him.

Eventually the crowd winds down to just those staying in the house and Aryn comes over to me. "It's time for bed," I tell him.

He nods. "All of a sudden I can hardly hold my head up," he tells me.

"You've crashed," I remind him. "It's normal and with everything else today, you've hit your limit."

He nods again in understanding and we proceed with saying our goodnights. Derek leads us into the house, giving us the brief tour Cotah was supposed to give us, but she went to bed more than an hour ago.

The house Derek has is gorgeous, very typical style for up here. Log cabin walls, wooden stairs and railings, it's gorgeous.

He leads us upstairs and down one of the hallways. "We'll go into details tomorrow, but next to the master suite, this is the next largest room. There's a bathroom in there along with enough closet space. If you need anything, let me know. I've got a lot of work to catch up on," he says.

"I'm sorry, Sir," Aryn offers.

Derek looks at him with sympathy. "Nonsense, boy. You don't need to apologize for anything."

Aryn nods his head slowly.

Derek turns to me and says, "My office is off the living room downstairs, if you need anything at all, I'll be in there."

"Thank you, Derek."

"Good night, you two." He smiles and heads back downstairs.

I usher Aryn inside. "Shower," I tell him and he nods before heading to his suitcase. I follow him and go to my own. We both pull out our kits and he strips out of his clothes. My cock hardens at his nakedness, but I notice he's soft. I let him go ahead of me so I can calm down my erection before climbing in the shower with him.

"Cay?" he calls from the doorway. I look over to him, our eyes meet. "Are you coming?"

I nod. "I just need a minute." Sadness creeps into his features. "I'm hard, Aryn," I explain to him. "I'm going to let him settle down before I come into the shower with you."

My eyes wander down his body and his cock hardens.

"I like that my body turns you on." He winks before disappearing into the bathroom.

"Greedy," I mumble and I hear his soft laugh from the bathroom.

I strip out of my clothes, my cock growing harder by the second as I walk into the bathroom where Aryn turns on the shower.

We didn't leave the shower for an hour after that.

Something wakes me up.

It takes a minute for me to realize what it is.

Aryn is shivering uncontrollably next to me. My eyes land on the clock. It's nearly four in the morning. I roll over, wrapping my arms around him. He has all the covers on top of him and yet he's still shivering. I try and blanket his body as much as I can and he starts awake.

"Why am I so cold?" he says through chattering teeth.

"I'm not sure, baby," I tell him. I rack my brain for anything that I've done that could have caused this and I'm come up blank.

I roll away from him and he starts shivering again. I grab my phone quickly and pull up Derek's number. "You alright?" he asks into the phone.

"Subdrop?"

"Yeah, what about it?"

"What happens, physically?"

"Depends on the person, but it usually happens within a few hours, why?"

"Aryn's shivering uncontrollably up here and it has nothing to do with the temperature in the room."

"I'll send Cotah in."

"No, don't wake her. What do I need to do?"

"She's already awake and on her way. I'll be there in a minute." He disconnects the call just as there's a timid knock on the door.

"Come in," I say and Cotah steps through the door.

"Is he talking?" Cotah asks me.

"I'm fine, darlin'. Just freezing," Aryn says and Cotah climbs on the bed.

I touch her shoulder. "He won't hurt me," she says softly as if reading my mind. I nod and she snuggles next to Aryn. "Sir, snuggle behind him," she says to me and I do. Aryn does his best to relax,

161

seeking permission from me to wrap his arms around Cotah, I nod to him and he does. He pulls her close and I pull them both even closer to me.

In all my time in the lifestyle, I've never experienced anything like this before. Sure, I've had subs have minor meltdowns the day following a scene, but that usually involved spending a little more time with them or I would focus on better aftercare the next time. Aryn's been through so much in the last twenty-four hours and I just want to love him, hold him close and keep him there.

Derek comes into the room and he has Teddy with him. Teddy has a smirk on his face. "Lit him up good, did ya?" he says and I roll my eyes. "He's droppin'."

"What do I do?" I ask him.

He smiles wider. "Exactly what you're doing. Snuggle him. Cotah will help."

"Is this gonna happen all the time?" Aryn says through chattering teeth.

"Nah, boy. You've had one hell of a fucked up day. You're riding a huge wave of adrenaline. This is your body's reaction to dumping it. Aftercare will almost always handle it, which I know Caden did, but given the hour of my phone call today, I don't imagine he had much time to deal," Teddy adds.

After what seems like forever but is really only a short while, Aryn's violent shivers settle into random ones.

"He's gonna be tired as hell when this is over," Teddy says. "What time's the appointment tomorrow?"

"We're supposed to pick up his sister tomorrow at eleven," I tell him.

"He might be up by then." Teddy nods.

"If not?"

"Just let him sleep," Derek adds.

I nod again and snuggle into Aryn. Gradually his shivers settle and run out completely, in the meantime Cotah fell asleep under Aryn.

"Poor girl can't keep her eyes open to save her life." Derek smiles at her then looks over at me. "You good?"

"I am, thank you for letting her help."

"Anytime. She's a lot warmer now that she's pregnant. Figured it would be the fastest way to warm him up."

"It worked," I whispered.

He scoops up his wife in his arms and she snuggles into him. The tank top she's wearing has slid up to under her breasts and I see her belly and my heart beats faster. The conversation Aryn and I had earlier about family and moving forward replays in my mind at the prospect of trying to have a family some way, somehow and after seeing him with Alyce tonight? I can't say no to him. Yes, she's an adult, but she's the only true family he has left.

It's with that thought that I drift back to sleep wrapped around Aryn, the love of my life, my world, my family and I realize that I will do anything to give him the world.

CHAPTER TWENTY-SIX

The days after my first experience with subdrop flew by in a whirlwind of madness.

I slept until one in the afternoon the next day. Thankfully Caden had found Alyce's number in my phone and called to let her know we would be late. Eventually we made it to the funeral home and the arrangements were made. Mom was buried that Tuesday and I was surrounded by my adoptive family. Caden was a rock for me through the whole thing. I'd managed to stave off my crazy crying jag until we were alone in our room that night. He was patient and gracious the entire time. At one point he was worried enough that he nearly dragged me into Derek's makeshift playroom in the lodge just to help me cope with what was happening to me.

Burying my mom was bittersweet. Her service was nice and Jason surprised me with his appreciation, not only of me, but of Caden.

That night, Alyce packed her bags, much to Alyx's chagrin, and came back to Derek's with Caden and me. She was going to move to Los Angeles and she was doing it without much of a fight. She said she was ready for something new. That night in Derek's house, she said she slept all night for the first time in more than a decade.

When I talked to her about it the next day, she said she knew that Jason would never hurt her again, but it was hard sleeping without one eye open nonetheless. Caden offered to help her with finding a therapist in Los Angeles that could help her work through her trauma. She was miffed at me for telling Caden her history, but she didn't stay that way for long. I think in the end, she knew just how traumatic it was for me as well as her.

Derek and Cotah's hospitality was unparalleled and I vowed to find a way to pay them back one day. Though I didn't know how to do that exactly. I learned from conversations that Cotah had lost her mother when she was young and that right before she'd met Derek

in Las Vegas, she'd lost her grandmother, the woman who was like a mother to her. My heart hurt for her, much the way hers hurt for me. She explained that her mother wasn't much of one either. Choosing drugs over her daughter. I'm not sure what hurt me more, the fact that my mother was a complete bitch or that Cotah had to grow up with something like that.

I'd filled Alyce in on Cotah's past and I told her that no matter where we come from, we choose where we go from there.

It's now Thanksgiving.

Caden's movie is officially done and ready to release early next year. He's so excited about this one and I can't say I blame him. During many nights of late work, he let me sit with him while he did what he needed to do, so I got a chance to see what he did for a living. It was exhilarating and I understood why he enjoyed it so much.

Caden and I are hosting Thanksgiving this year and we're doing it with a huge family around us. My adoptive family and my sister.

Addison, Talon, Kyle and the twins, Calvin, Eric and their good friend Jessica - rumor has it that Jessica is going to surrogate for the guys and that warms my heart to no end. Those two have been through enough in their lives, they deserve everything they could possibly want. Dex and Raine are coming. Raine found out shortly after the funeral that her and Dex would be expecting their first child in the spring. I was over the moon with happiness for them. Since then they've put the condo - Addison's old place - on the market and have found a house not far from Caden and I. Casey, along with Mills, Rusty and Victoria will be here too. I've told them that working is off limits, but if I know Mills, he won't turn it off long enough to enjoy the meal.

Derek and Cotah are coming from North Carolina. The girl looks like she's about to pop but she's making the trip. When I invited them, she said they'd be here with bells on.

Cami, Tristan and their son Jayden are coming from Phoenix and

they're bringing their friends, Ireland and Dyson, with them. I've had the pleasure of meeting them and Ireland is a hoot, I'm excited to see her again.

Alyce is over the moon at joining me for our first Thanksgiving together in ten years. I can't disagree with her.

Oh, and we have one more important guest coming.

Ashley.

After my massive subdrop and the funeral was over, I found the courage to explain what that night meant to me. Up until then, I'd hid it pretty well so that he wouldn't ask me questions. He was pretty pissed that I waited so long to tell him about it, but in the end, he understood.

I admitted to him that I miss the softness of a woman in my arms. He agreed with me and while we haven't made any major decisions about bringing a woman into our relationship, we've talked extensively about it.

In the end, we both agreed that neither one of us was fully comfortable with just a surrogate. Given that Cay and I both come from hetero-relationship backgrounds, we understand the importance of the woman's role in something like that. Regardless, decisions aren't going to be made for some time, but we mutually agreed that if we were going to bring in anyone, it would be Ash. Who knows, maybe we will decide on something else, but for now, I'm beyond happy with the new life we're creating together.

On Halloween, at Addison, Talon and Kyle's house, Caden proposed to me. Of course I said yes. We're planning a spring wedding.

The day after Halloween found us flying to Nashville and Caden promptly took me to The Box where he collared me, officially, in front of everyone. My hand brushes the chain around my neck. It's similar to the one he had given me as a training collar, but it's a little shorter and there's a small inscription that says, My love, my life, my heart, my body, my mind, my soul forever," on it. Caden wears one

similar to mine around his neck with the same inscription inside it.

I never take it off and neither does he.

He comes up behind me as I'm standing at the counter and he wraps his arms around my waist before kissing me on my shoulder. "What are you thinking about so hard?" he asks and I simply scoot my butt back into his crotch. His cock hardens instantly and he nips at my ear. "Behave, my sweet little slut, or I will take you over this counter," he growls.

I wiggle my hips at him again and he pulls away, smacking my ass, hard. I moan. "My insatiable slut."

I turn around and wrap my arms around him. "Always yours."

"Forever," he says before claiming my lips with his own.

My body melts into his and I groan into his mouth as my cock tries to harden, but it can't and I grunt in pain. Caden pulls back and gives me a knowing smirk. "I warned you about that smart mouth of yours, pet."

My eyes flutter downward. "Yes, Master," I breathe and my cock settles.

He presses into me and his erection presses into me. "Just think of how sweet it will be when I take that off of you tonight and suck your cock so far into my mouth you won't know what to do with yourself."

I shudder at his words. "Oh yes, Master."

He presses his forehead against mine. "I love you, Aryn."

"I love you, Caden."

This is my happy place.

A few months ago I was a wandering manwhore who never believed he could find true love. Now, not only am I his willing slave, but he's my Master. He brought me to my knees and became the absolute love of my life.

He's my home.

My life.

My love.

And everything I've ever dreamed of all rolled into one beautiful package.

I'm at his mercy.

I'm at Caden's command and I've never been happier in my entire life.

EIGHTEEN MONTHS LATER

*S*ix months ago, I moved to California, and though it was only meant to be temporary, I'm not sure I see myself leaving anytime soon.

I moved in with Aryn and Master Caden at their behest. I wanted to get my own apartment and find a job, but Caden insisted I move in with them and let him take care of me.

And boy have they ever.

Our relationship is strictly platonic. No sex, no D/S play, just really close friends. Though I must admit, the lack of sex is hard, especially now.

My hand slides over the small bump protruding from my midsection.

My moving here meant that I agreed to be their surrogate. It wasn't an easy decision to make, especially since I'm only twenty-six years old and I've yet to meet someone of my own. These two were incredibly hard to say no to. Not that I was forced, not by any stretch of the imagination, but I've been assured over and over that I would be taken care of, not only during my pregnancy, but afterward too.

The one concession I made and the two of them agreed to, is that I get to be a part of the child's life, for the rest of its life. Neither one of them objected. Not only am I carrying their child, but they are using my egg, therefore, I am its biological mother.

That hadn't been part of the original plan, but after we did all the testing required by our fertility doctor, there was no reason we couldn't have conceived this child naturally. Instead, I was artificially inseminated. Neither myself, nor Aryn or Caden, know who the biological father is. They wanted it that way and it makes me happy.

While also making me cry, and puke and ache everywhere.

I'm only four months along, but still, my boobs hurt, my back is

starting to ache and though the morning sickness has subsided for the most part, I still have an occasional bout with it.

The door to my room opens and I don't turn around. It's morning and I already know who it is. He walks across the room to where I'm standing at the window looking out over the ocean. There's a gentle breeze coming in bringing the scent of sun and beach with it.

Warm hands slide around my midsection and land gently on my stomach. "How are you feeling?" Aryn asks me.

"Good," I smile and nod.

"No puking?" he asks.

I chuckle, "Not yet."

"Good."

I know what he wants next so I turn in his arms and he kneels before me. He lifts my tank top and places a gentle kiss on the lower swell of my belly and I smile at him. I can't help gingerly running my hand through his growing locks atop his head and he smiles, then whispers to my belly.

I do my best to tune out what he or Caden says when they have their time with the baby because it is their baby and the more I listen, the more I fall in love with the two of them.

When Aryn finishes his one-sided conversation with my belly, he kisses me again and stands. He kisses me on the cheek and murmurs his thank you in my ear.

In about an hour, Caden will find me and do the same.

Then after dinner, the three of us sit on the couch and they both have their moment together with my bump. Those moments are getting harder because their obvious love for the little one growing inside me warms my heart and usually sends tears to my eyes. I blame hormones, but the reality is, I hope to one day find a man who appreciates me the way these two do.

Between the two of them, they make no secret of helping me find my One.

Caden took me under his wing of protection in the lifestyle scene here in California. Going to the club, even though I'm not showing, is still one of my favorite things to do. There are a couple of Tops at the club we attend that Caden has given his permission, albeit with a laundry list of rules, to play with me.

I look forward to those nights because it gives me a chance to feel normal, to find my happy place. When it's over, the Top provides me with aftercare until the boys bring me home, then they provide me with even more.

How am I supposed to survive this and not get hurt in the end?

I have no idea.

Eventually, I will have to find a way to do so.

Seeing Aryn and Caden together is a happy place all by itself. They are so in love with each other that it only makes me long for something half as strong as what they have.

Caden comes in my room. I wipe the tears from my eyes quickly, hoping he doesn't see them. "What's wrong?" he asks, his voice concerned.

I shake my head and rub my hand over my belly again. "I'm fine," I tell him. "Stupid hormones," I mutter.

"That answer is getting old, girl." His tone is that of the Dominant man I fell in love with a couple years ago and I shiver.

"I'm sorry, Sir, I...it's really stupid," I tell him.

"Nothing is stupid, love." His voice is softer as he wraps his arms around me from behind, his hands resting atop mine on my belly.

"This is really stupid."

"Tell me," he whispers, but that command is there.

I let out a laughing sob and catch my breath. "I'm really fucking horny," I groan.

Caden chuckles behind me then releases a hand from my belly and brings his phone in front of both of us. He finds Aryn's name and sends a text:

Come to Ashley's room, my sweet slut.

I learned early on that Caden calling Aryn his sweet slut is Caden's way of letting Aryn know that it's not casual time.

Within a moment, Aryn is in the room.

"What's wrong?" he asks and I blush like an idiot.

"I think it's time we take care of our girl," Caden says and Aryn's face lights up with the biggest smile I've ever seen him wear.

"What are you..." I don't say anything else because Caden's hands slide up my belly, cupping my swollen sensitive tits in his palms. "Oh god," I moan when Aryn kneels before me.

"We promised to take care of you, any way you needed," Aryn says with a wink as he reaches for my pajama shorts. His hands are soft, warm and my pussy ignites in a desire unlike anything I've ever felt before.

My heart explodes.

I'm not going to survive this pregnancy in one piece.

The next thing I know, Caden's fingers are rolling my taut nipples and Aryn's hand is sliding through my slick sex. The rest of the world falls away.

The End

ABOUT THE AUTHOR

BEST SELLING Erotic, Paranormal and Contemporary Romance author Zoey Derrick comes from Glendale, Arizona. Zoey, was a mortgage underwriter by day and is now a romance and erotica novelist full-time. She writes stories as hot as the desert sun itself. It is this passion that drips off of her work, bringing excitement to anyone who enjoys a good and sensual love story.

Not only does she aim to take her readers on an erotic dance that lasts the night, it allows her to empty her mind of stories we all wish were true.

Her stories are hopeful yet true to life, skillfully avoiding melodrama and the unrealistic, bringing her gripping Erotica only closer to the heart of those that dare dipping into it.

The intimacy of her fantasies that she shares with her readers is thrilling and encouraging, climactic yet full of suspense. She is a loving mistress, up for anything, of which any reader is doomed to return to again and again

DID YOU KNOW...

That several of the couples you've met in this book have their own stories...

CAMI & TRISTAN
With Cami and Tristan's story you will meet - Beau & Mick,
Travis & Naomi and Jolene & Tyson

Finding Love's Wings
Chasing Love's Wings

DEREK & DACOTAH
One Week

ADDISON, TALON, & KYLE
Claiming Addison
Craving Talon
Redeeming Kyle

DEX & RAINE
Taming Dex
Devouring Raine

CALVIN & ERIC (MOUSE & PEACOCK)
Defining Us

ARYN & CADEN
Aryn's Desire
Caden's Command (Coming Soon)

HAPPY READING!